Melani
l

MW01047080

Melanie Bluelake's Dream

Betty Dorion

Coteau Books

Edited by Peter Carver.
Cover painting, *Melanie Bluelake's Dream*, watercolor on gouache, by Sherry Farrell Racette
Cover and book design by Val Jakubowski.
Typeset by Val Jakubowksi.
Printed and bound in Canada.

The publisher gratefully acknowledges the financial assistance of the Saskatchewan Arts Board, the Canada Council, the Department of Canadian Heritage, and the City of Regina Arts Commission.

Canadian Cataloguing in Publication Data

Dorion, Betty, 1952-

Melanie Bluelake's Dream

ISBN 1-55050-081-3

I. Title.

PS8557.075M4 1995   jC813'.54   C95-920020-7
PZ7.D67Me 1995

06432

COTEAU BOOKS
401-2206 Dewdney Avenue
Regina, SK
S4R 1H3

To my husband, John

Table of Contents

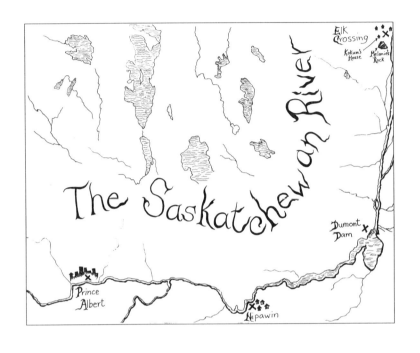

*A glossary of the Cree words used in this story
can be found at the end of the book.*

Departure

*T*he day had the look and feel of miserable right from the start.

A black sky leaned over the spruce trees. The raw wind smacked Melanie in the face and tugged at her tight braid. She was down at the river one last time. During the past few days she had cried enough tears to raise the water level.

Melanie braced herself against her rock. Bigger than *Kōhkom*'s porch, it gave her shelter but no warmth. Sharp needles of cold pricked her arms and legs.

She stayed until she was ready to leave. Until she felt the strength of the river, metal grey this morning, seep into her bones. The river always gave her what she needed. Today it toughened her, steeled her to be able to say goodbye to *Kōhkom*.

Two hours later, as she slumped in the back seat of the taxivan, the image of *Kōhkom*'s heavy shape sagging against the porch door lingered in her mind. In the end Melanie had been the strong one, draping her skinny arms over *Kōhkom*'s soft shoulders and whispering in her grandmother's ear, "I'll be back, *Kōhkom*, I promise." She'd tightened her arms. "Before you know it."

Melanie glared again at the front of the van. Her mother sat across from Harve, the driver, chatting and laughing. She probably hadn't given *Kōhkom* a second thought since they left Elk Crossing several hours ago. Melanie was disgusted.

She flipped open the notepad Keena had given her. On the first page Keena had made a list: *Why You'll Always Be My Best Friend*. They'd been doing stuff like that in school, and she and Keena had written about each other.

Although Melanie knew the list by heart, she read again the nice things Keena had written, about how kind she was and how she thought up fun things to do. At the bottom of the page was the part she liked best. Keena had ended by saying that they would be *Best Friends Forever*. Scrunching down in the seat Melanie covered her face with the notepad, holding back hot tears that burned her eyelids.

The van hit a deep pothole and Melanie bounced on her seat. Her mother called back to her, "Are you all right, my girl?" Melanie ignored her and smoothed out the sheet of paper before turning the page. She stabbed her pencil at the paper, forming thick dark words:

Why I Hate My Mom

1. *Without even asking me how I felt* she decided to go back to school (in the city).
2. Then she says I have to go too.
3. She and *Kōhkom* get into a big argument and *Kōhkom* gets one of her bad headaches. *All Mom's fault!*
4. After *Kōhkom* gets better she and Mom have a talk. *Without me. Which means I have no say.*
5. Mom *somehow* gets *Kōhkom* on her side. Which means *again I have no say* and have to go with Mom.

Underneath she scribbled in large messy letters:

But I don't have to like it !!!

She was going to let her mom know just how she felt.

When the time was right.

School

*T*he bell had rung a full five minutes ago. Still Melanie waited outside the school's heavy double doors. Alone. It was her own fault.

Slouched against the building, she shivered as much from dread as from the cold. She cupped her hands around her eyes and peered through the thick window. The entrance had cleared of the last latecomers. She checked the street once more. No one else in sight.

Her mother had wanted to come with her. But Melanie shook her head. "I don't need you," she had said, punching the words into her mother's face. Then, before her mom could reply, she'd walked out, letting the door slam behind her.

Now she wished that she hadn't been so

quick in turning down the offer. She shook her head to get rid of the thought. The long thick braid hanging down her back barely moved.

Heaving a sigh, she hunched her thin shoulders and tugged halfheartedly on the oversized handle, opening the door just wide enough to slip through. Then, hands braced behind her back, she eased it shut again. Inside, a big red arrow directed her up the stairs to the principal's office. Hugging the wall, Melanie followed it until she came to an open door on her left.

There was no one at the desk directly in front of her. Melanie looked through a glass partition to an inner office. There a man was leaning over an open drawer of a filing cabinet. He looked up.

Melanie couldn't breathe. Her chest felt like someone was sitting on her. She pretended she hadn't seen him.

Coming out of his office the man said, "Hi, I'm Mr. Mooney. I'm the principal."

Melanie's eyes examined a dirty spot on the ugly brown carpet. She said nothing.

"Are you alone?" he asked, walking past her and peering down the stairs.

Melanie waited.

The principal turned back to her. "I guess you are," he said, stuffing his hands into his pockets and bending over her so that he was looking right in her face. "Well then, what can I do for you?"

Melanie edged back until she'd put a distance between them. She hated his voice, so kind and concerned. She knew that if she spoke one word the tears would come. And she wasn't about to let that happen.

"Come in and sit down," he said, standing aside for her to enter his office.

Looking straight ahead, Melanie marched past him. She flicked her braid around to her back and perched on the edge of the chair by his huge wooden desk.

The principal sat down and leaned towards

her. In an even gentler tone he asked, "Do you want to register for school?"

Melanie pulled back from him and gripped the sides of the chair so hard her knuckles whitened. If she was going to get through this, he'd better drop the sympathy. She nodded in answer to his question, her mouth tightly closed and her dark eyes roving the room.

Mr. Mooney picked up a pen. "You're a brave girl to come to a new school all by yourself. Your mom couldn't come with you today?"

Melanie knew he was waiting for her to say something. She shook her head and mumbled, "She's busy."

The principal pulled a yellow form out of a side drawer and scribbled something across the top. "Well," he said, "can you help me fill this out?"

Melanie looked at the paper, but in her mind she mimicked him. Of course she could, if she chose to. In fact, she could save him the trouble and fill out the darn thing herself.

Mr. Mooney continued, "Your name?"

She brought her eyes back to the yellow form and said, "I can fill it out myself." The minute the words were out she knew she'd sounded like a smart mouth. But it was the truth. She shifted on the chair and tucked a loose strand of hair behind her ear, waiting for him to say something. She wished the guy would keep his eyes to himself.

"Fine," the principal agreed, a little too heartily, Melanie thought. He slid the sheet and a pen across to her, then hesitated as if he were going to say something. But he seemed to change his mind, and turned his attention to a mound of papers on the other end of his desk.

Melanie eyed him from under her lashes until she was sure he was no longer watching her. Then she concentrated on the form, filling the blanks with her best handwriting. She didn't know why she bothered. She sure wasn't trying to impress him.

The top part of the page was easy. Melanie Bluelake, she wrote; on the next blank, *ten years old*. Birthdate: October 23. Last school attended? Easy. Elk Crossing Elementary. She was pretty sure she spelled elementary right. She checked the blank next to the words, lives with mother. It looked more like an angry slash than a check. She left it. Then she came to the part she didn't know, her address in the city and other stuff.

She cleared her throat. "We're staying with

my mom's friend. Her name is Lorraine," she said, eyes fixed on the yellow form. "My mom is looking for her own place." In her mind she excluded herself from the whole notion.

Mr. Mooney nodded. "Here, let me see." He reached for the form. Melanie slid it towards him. "What is Lorraine's last name?"

"Mackenzie," Melanie replied, noticing he wrote it on the top of the form and not in one of the blank spaces.

"Does she have any children?" Mr. Mooney asked.

Melanie nodded.

"Any in school?"

She shook her head. She didn't know how old the two little boys were, but one was still in diapers and the other would go to school the next year, she had heard Lorraine tell her mom last night.

Melanie felt the principal's eyes on her. She picked at a scab on her knuckle.

Finally, he spoke. "Will you bring Lorraine's address with you tomorrow, Melanie? We need it so we can contact your mother in case of an emergency, like if you get sick."

Melanie nodded. He tore off the top copy of the registration form and handed it to her. "You can take this home. Ask your mom to complete as much as she can." The principal stood up. "Come with me," he said, "I'll take you to your room."

Melanie looked down at the cold clammy hands she clutched in her lap. The chill she felt had nothing to do with the thin summer jacket she wore this cool October morning. Her mouth was dry as stale bannock. She swallowed; it didn't help.

She stood up to go with the principal, her hands clenched into fists in her pockets and her eyes lowered so she wouldn't have to look at him. She shied away from the hand he was about to lay on her shoulder. As they walked down the stairs she tried to stay a bit behind him so she wouldn't have to talk, but the principal matched his pace to hers.

"Have you been to Prince Albert before?"

A slight shake of her head that meant no.

They walked down a long grey hallway, plastered on both sides with drawings of odd looking Thanksgiving turkeys and horns of plenty spilling harvest vegetables down the concrete wall. Melanie looked, just to have somewhere to put her eyes. The art looked familiar, like the stuff the kids in Elk Crossing did.

"*Mōniyās* art," Uncle Pierre had commented once. When she'd asked why he said, "When was the last time you saw an Indian celebrate Thanksgiving?" He had chuckled through his cigarette smoke. But he was right. Melanie thought about it later. Only the white people from outside, like the teachers and nurses and RCMP, made a big deal of Thanksgiving. After that, she never did any turkey art. She could still see Miss Critch's poppy eyes and her slack jaw when she told her why. And she could also see the shocked look on Keena's face! At recess she told the whole playground what Melanie had done. She would never have a friend like Keena here.

Mr. Mooney broke into her thoughts. "Pretty snazzy art, eh?"

Melanie knew he was trying to get a response from her. But she wouldn't smile, wouldn't talk. She hadn't wanted to leave home, hadn't wanted to come to this school. As far as she was concerned, there was nothing to talk about, nothing to smile about.

The principal stopped in front of one of the grey doors. Melanie shrank back against the wall, her legs as wobbly as the time she'd danced all evening at her cousin Pauline's wedding. She wasn't dancing now.

Mr. Mooney straightened a droopy store-bought cardboard turkey and pressed it back against a wad of tape.

Melanie waited, her breathing laboured, like she was under a heavy blanket.

Then he knocked on the door and poked his head inside.

She stiffened and closed her eyes for a second to block it all out. From inside the room the kids called to him. They sounded so loud and there seemed to be so many of them. Her stomach dropped at the thought of going in there.

A young girl came to the door. This couldn't be the teacher! She didn't look any older than Melanie's cousin Sharon in Grade 12 back in Elk Crossing. But Mr. Mooney handed her a copy of the registration form and said, "This is Melanie Bluelake, from Elk Crossing."

Melanie felt the pressure of the principal's hand on her back nudging her forward. "Melanie, this is your teacher, Miss Ryan."

Melanie hung back, resenting his hand and his pleasant voice. But there was no escaping the teacher. Hands outstretched, Miss Ryan came so close she was practically standing on Melanie's toes. Flustered, Melanie stepped back. But the teacher, hardly taller than she, grasped

Melanie's arm and beamed into her face. "Hi, Melanie. Welcome to our class."

Melanie turned her head aside, away from the young teacher's friendly blue eyes. She moved her arm so that the teacher's hand rested only on the sleeve of her jacket.

As the principal left them he said, "I'll ask Mr. Impey to bring you a desk."

"Good," the teacher replied, finally removing her hand from Melanie's jacket. "And I think I have extra textbooks." She turned back to Melanie and tilted her head to look right in Melanie's face. "Are you feeling shy?" she asked, flashing a kind smile. "I know it's hard to come to a new school. But it won't be long before you'll have lots of friends."

Melanie chewed the inside of her lip, trying to stop its nervous trembling. She felt like telling the teacher she didn't want lots of friends, at least not here. She didn't plan on being around that long. Instead, she tucked that loose strand of hair behind her ear again, evading the hand the teacher had been about to lay on her shoulder.

"Come on in," Miss Ryan said, "we'll get you settled."

Melanie jammed her hands deep in her jacket pockets to control the shaking she couldn't stop.

There was a ripping sound from the lining inside. She trailed after the teacher into the noisy room.

Rachel – and Tanya

"*B*oys and girls!"

Nobody seemed to hear the teacher. Melanie rocked back and forth on her ankles. What now, she wondered.

Her eyes took in Miss Ryan's frustrated face, flushed as pink as a trout's belly. With an agitated movement the teacher pushed her short straight hair off her forehead. A few strands stuck up on her head and stayed there. If Melanie hadn't been so nervous she would have laughed.

Miss Ryan planted one hand on her hip. With a determined set to her chin she clicked the light switch off and on, rising to her tiptoes as she did so. Finally, the din subsided enough for her to call, "Boys and girls, remember our discussion. If you waste my time, I'll have to waste yours at recess."

The teacher sounded as if she wanted to be stern but hadn't quite figured out yet how to go about it. Melanie was surprised that the noise dwindled except for a few whispers and giggles, mostly from the back of the room.

"I'd like you to meet Melanie Bluelake...." The teacher ploughed on. But Melanie heard only the quiet, and hated being the reason for it. Stares, from at least a hundred pairs of eyes it seemed, bored into her.

Then, mustering a calm she didn't feel, Melanie turned her back to them. She took her time hanging her jacket on the coat rack. Funny, she hadn't noticed before how faded her pink coat was. *They* probably noticed it right away. Well, let them.

Miss Ryan hovered over her while the class waited and watched. "I taught a boy from Elk Crossing last year," she said, smoothing down her boyish hairdo. "His name is Bradley Wolfe. Do you know him?"

Melanie nodded her head once, fixing her eyes on the scuffed toes of her runners. She knew Bradley. He'd been in her class in Elk Crossing. If she'd had any luck she would still be there too, sitting right across from Keena.

Miss Ryan, chattering like a magpie, took some paper from a shelf and handed it to her along with a pencil. "You can sit at the round table at the back of the room until your desk arrives." She spoke to a girl sitting near the front. "Rachel, will you sit with Melanie?" The teacher turned her sunshine smile on Melanie again, and there was the hand on Melanie's shoulder. "Rachel will help you."

Melanie looked neither right nor left as she walked to the table. But she knew every head turned and followed her. And she felt every nosy look. The paper the teacher had given her lay blank before her, just as blank as she felt. At least the teacher had the sense to put her in the back of the room. Here she could stare down anyone who wanted to gawk at her.

The girl called Rachel picked up her paper and pencil and made her way to Melanie's table. Melanie watched her ponytail bounce as she walked down the row. This girl was really short. Rachel slid onto the next chair and curled her feet under her. A shy, uncertain grin flickered across her face. Melanie didn't smile back.

They did math first, writing big numbers like millions. The teacher glanced at Melanie's paper as she walked down the rows. Melanie knew she was trying to see if this work was difficult for her. She breathed easier after the teacher passed. She guessed she knew just as much as these kids – so far anyway.

She sneaked a few looks around the room. She noticed that while most of her classmates were Indian, a few were white. She wondered if they spoke Cree, or if any of them had moved in from the North like her. They looked like they belonged here. Well, she didn't. She belonged at home, with *Kōhkom*. She clenched the teacher's pencil tight in her hand.

Melanie couldn't remember a time when she and her mom hadn't lived with *Kōhkom*. Until now. When she was younger she loved to listen to *Kōhkom*'s stories about when she was a tiny baby. *Kōhkom* took care of her so her mom could go to the city to finish high school. But she didn't finish. She was too lonely for Elk Crossing.

After her mom returned they lived with her dad for a while, her mom had told her. It didn't work out, and her dad moved to Vancouver and married someone else there. Melanie didn't care. She didn't know him anyway. And *Kōhkom* didn't seem to think much of him. The few times his name was mentioned, *Kōhkom* just shook her head.

She couldn't figure why her mom had to go back to school. She already worked a couple days a week at the store in Elk Crossing. Lots of people on the reserve didn't have any work.

When recess came, Rachel, at the teacher's suggestion, rushed Melanie through a quick tour of the school. "We'll skip the classrooms," she said, "they're all alike anyway." She looked up at Melanie, her face a question. "Unless you want to?"

Melanie shook her head, hardly more than a twitch. She watched Rachel, a half step ahead of her, noticing that the other girl's head came up only about as far as her nose. Everything about Rachel was tiny, right down to her feet. Melanie felt big and tall next to her.

Rachel flitted down the hall toward the girls' washroom. She stopped in the doorway and wrinkled her nose. "Stinks in here," she said.

Melanie noticed wads of paper towel on the floor all around the garbage can. She followed Rachel around the corner and down a set of stairs.

Rachel looked up at her. "Do you like Miss Ryan?" she asked.

Melanie shrugged.

"I do," Rachel went on. "She's really nice. Do

you know this is her first year teaching? She told us."

Rachel didn't seem to expect a reply. The stairs led to a crowded library. They peered in the door before taking a different set of steps up to the gym.

Melanie knew she'd never be able to find any of these places by herself. She saw nothing that impressed her. She had thought the city school would be newer, but her school in Elk Crossing was just as good, she thought smugly.

Rachel hadn't waited for comments along the way and Melanie hadn't offered any. But as she followed Rachel back down the stairs from the gym, she felt she owed her something. "It's bigger than my school," Melanie said.

Rachel nodded in understanding. "When I moved here, I got lost lots of times." She laughed, and lowered her voice. "One day I was trying to find the bathroom, and I walked into the janitor's room," she said.

Melanie smiled, in spite of herself. "What happened?"

Rachel shrugged, her mouth still in a wide grin. "Nothing," she said. "He wasn't there."

They rounded a corner and Rachel steered Melanie towards the door. "*Kinipa*, Melanie, recess is half over. Let's go to the swinging bridge."

Melanie's mouth dropped open. "You know Cree?" she squeaked, grabbing Rachel's arm.

Without breaking her stride Rachel replied, "Some. Do you?"

Melanie's head bobbed up and down. "*Ēhē*," she replied. "I speak Cree all the time at home."

"I can count ..." Using her fingers Rachel started, "*pēyak, nīso, nisto, nēwo, niyānan* ..." Just as she got to five the bell rang. Rachel screwed up her face; her long bangs hung in her eyes. "We just got out here," she groaned, as the playground teacher shooed them toward the door. Rachel continued rattling off the Cree numbers to ten.

Melanie corrected her. "Not *tepagoke*. Say *tē pakōhp*."

As the kids entered the building they removed their outside runners and placed them on the boot rack just inside the door. Melanie leaned against the wall. If she took hers off she would be in her bare feet. She didn't have indoor runners.

She saw Miss Ryan fight her way against the current of kids cramming the hallway as they waited, restless and loud, for their teachers to unlock classroom doors. Unable to break through the throng, Miss Ryan called over their heads, "Melanie, keep your runners on for today. I'll give you a supply list before you go home."

The class settled into their desks. Two boys, starting at opposite sides of the room, walked up and down the rows, slapping a napkin in front of each student. Melanie watched, curious.

"It's snack time," Rachel whispered. "See?" She puckered her lips and jutted her chin toward the front of the room where Miss Ryan held a large tray of muffins and cheese. But it was Rachel Melanie watched. She was chinning! Just like a real Cree. Melanie grinned. She knew Rachel thought it was because of the muffins.

"Anyone with runners done up gets to choose a muffin first," the teacher announced. Melanie thought she looked proud of herself for having such a good idea. Kids wrestled with runners and laces.

Melanie had hers on but she didn't want to be the first to put her hand up.

She was starving, though. Her insides rumbled. She pressed her hands against her stomach to stop the noise before somebody heard. There'd been only bread at Lorraine's this morning, not even any butter. Just a scrape of storebought jam in the bottom of a messy jar. She'd refused to eat. The satisfaction she'd felt at having her mother practically beg her to eat a piece of toast felt hollow now. Like her stomach.

Melanie downed the blueberry muffin and cheese. She and *Kōhkom* had picked lots of blueberries last summer. She stabbed at a berry left on her napkin and kept her eyes wide open, determined not to blink. Finally the tears went away.

The class groaned when the teacher told them to take out their science books. "It's hard," Rachel informed Melanie. After reading a page about rock formations Melanie agreed. But at least the effort to understand the stuff wiped everything else from her mind.

She cringed when the noon bell rang. Rachel went to put her books away. Melanie turned her papers down on the table. Her work was nobody's business.

Miss Ryan leaned over her, her voice whispery. "Are you supposed to go home for lunch, Melanie?"

Melanie shrugged. She might, or she might not. She was surprised at her own daring. What could her mother do if she didn't go to Lorraine's for lunch? She really wasn't sure. At home *Kōhkom* did practically all the telling. Her mom had always been more like a nagging big sister.

One thing was for sure. She didn't want to go back to Lorraine's place. It was definitely not home, nowhere near it.

"Never mind. Come with me," said Miss Ryan, her hand on Melanie's chair.

Melanie pushed away from the table. Did this woman never give up? She wondered where they were going. Melanie followed her out the front door and across the street to a big building. Kids dribbled through the door in groups of two and three. The teacher stopped, her hand on the door handle, and turned to Melanie. "This is the church hall," she told her. "You can have lunch here."

Miss Ryan's hand on her back nudged her into the room. Melanie stopped short. This teacher was as bad as the principal. They must have gone to the same teacher school. Sick of being herded about, she roughly shrugged the teacher's hand away and edged closer to the door. She didn't want to eat here.

"It's okay, Melanie. Lots of kids come to the hall to eat." Her teacher caught her by the arm and beckoned to a woman across the room.

"Coming," the woman called, laying a plate of sandwiches in front of several kids. The plate emptied in zero time.

"This is Mrs. McKay," her teacher said. "She'll bring you lunch." To Mrs. McKay she added, "Melanie is new. Everything is confusing, I'm sure. Can you see that she's taken care of?"

Mrs. McKay smiled. "You know I will." She looked at Melanie. "*Ki-nēhinawān cī?*"

Melanie nodded in answer to her question, but her Cree was different from the Cree this woman spoke. "Sit anywhere you like," Mrs. McKay told her. "I'll be right back with your lunch."

Melanie sat at the end of the table, as far away as she could from the other kids. Mrs. McKay returned with a bowl of chicken noodle soup and a ham and cheese sandwich on bannock. Melanie's mouth watered. But she took her time eating. She wasn't going to let these kids see how hungry she was.

However, after a couple of mouthfuls

Melanie couldn't eat anymore. Her stomach churned with each lump of food she forced down; she felt awful. She wrapped the bannock in her napkin and poked it close to the side of the soup bowl. She watched Mrs. McKay bring more bannock to the noisy table and then snuck out the door while the woman's back was turned.

Once in the fresh air Melanie felt a little better. She stood at the curb watching cars pass, intrigued by how many vehicles there were. She half smiled at the thought of the dust this many cars would create back home. *Kōhkom* would hate it. She hated cars anyway and would get right off the road, practically standing in the bush when she heard a car coming. And she would just stand and wait until the car had passed! Melanie used to laugh at her. It was a good thing her grandmother wasn't here.

She sighed and pictured *Kōhkom* eating lunch. She was probably sitting down at the end of the table with her cup of tea right now. Feeling the tears burn her eyelids, Melanie sniffed noisily and rubbed her sleeve across her eyes, impatient with herself. Her eyes were as leaky as the rusty old tap on the water truck back home.

She shook her head to clear her thoughts and wandered across the street, wondering about those kids not having lunches. Why didn't they go to an auntie's house to eat? In Elk Crossing, if there was no one home Melanie would run to Auntie Elsie's or to Keena's house for lunch. This place was weird.

She wondered if her friend was walking back to school by herself today. Melanie had always stopped at Keena's house after lunch and they'd walked to school together.

An ear-splitting blast right beside her startled her. She shrieked, spooked by the suddenness of it. Scowling at the teenage boy driving a wreck of a car, she took her time moving out of the way. Her heart was still thumping as he roared off. She yelled after him. "Watch where you're going or I'll kick your headlight in!" Good thing his window was up or he might have come after her.

Melanie wheeled around at the sound of laughing behind her.

"Scared ya, huh?" chortled a frizzy-haired girl. She had obviously enjoyed the whole thing and was now snickering at Melanie's embarrassment.

"So?" Melanie shot back at her.

The smirk on the girl's face widened, showing eyeteeth sticking halfway out of her gums like fangs.

"What's it to you?" Melanie spat as she brushed past.

But she didn't have the last word. The girl called after her, "So you ate lunch at the hall, did you?"

Melanie made a face. Now what was that supposed to mean? The girl for sure wasn't being friendly.

Rachel called to her from an ancient green station wagon idling in front of the school. Waving goodbye to the woman at the wheel she ran up to Melanie. "That's Tanya," Rachel told her. "She's mean sometimes."

Melanie looked back over her shoulder as she followed Rachel to the swings in front of the school. Tanya's nasty green eyes had narrowed to slashes. The girl tossed her frizzy hair and stood looking after them with her hands on her hips.

Melanie flicked her braid. Who cares about her anyway? She pulled back on the tangled chain links of a broken swing and shoved it away again with all the force she could muster. She looked around. Like the school, the playground wasn't much different from Elk Crossing. She'd expected it to have fancy equipment, but she saw that it wasn't so. There were broken swings here too. Good.

And there was at least one mean kid.

Back in class Melanie looked at the back of the paper she'd turned down on the table before lunch. On it someone had scrawled the words:

I'll get you

There was no need to wonder who wrote it. Tanya stood at the pencil sharpener. With each grind she shot Melanie a nasty look.

Lies

*M*elanie and Tanya both had to stay behind after class.

Melanie waited for Miss Ryan to find a supply list.

Tanya had to finish her social studies map.

Melanie couldn't hide a smug grin at the sight of Tanya stewing at her desk. Too bad. She should have done her work when she had the chance.

The teacher passed Melanie the paper. "You probably have some of these things already," she said, flashing her sunshine smile again. At least this time she kept her hands to herself.

On the way out Melanie glanced at the list, partly out of curiosity, and partly because she was trying to ignore Tanya. It wasn't easy, with her muttering and sending menacing looks in

Melanie's direction when the teacher wasn't looking.

Melanie scanned the page and drew in her breath. What was all this stuff for? On the way to Lorraine's house, just down the street, she read through it.

1 pr. gym shoes (white soles for inside use)
10 pencils (HB)
1 ruler (30 cm. plastic or wood)
2 erasers (pink pearl)
1 eraser (pen/pencil)
1 scissors (good quality, pointed)
1 glue (bottle, white Lepage)
1 wax crayons (24, Laurentian)
1 pencil crayons (24, Crayola)
2 ballpoint pens (blue)
1 ballpoint pen (red)
1 pencil case
1 school bag or tote bag
1 Kleenex (large box)
8 duotangs
15 notebooks (Hilroy, ruled, 3 ring, no coil)
200 loose leaf sheets (lined)
1 dictionary (Winston Canadian)
1 recorder (Yamaha Soprano)

In her mind she checked the supplies she'd

brought with her. Not much, a couple note-books, pencils, and a ruler. She'd lost her eraser. Tomorrow she'd have to bring what she had.

She'd heard *Kōhkom* tell her mother her old runners would have to last until it was time to buy winter boots. Now she'd need new runners and new boots. Served her mother right. Maybe she would change her tune about living in the city after seeing this list. Melanie couldn't wait to see the look on her face.

Not only was the list twice as long as hers had been back home, but much of the stuff had to be a special kind. Back home as long as you had a notebook nobody cared what kind it was. And every classroom had their own glue, scissors, and set of dictionaries, so nobody had to buy them.

Melanie stopped on the sidewalk to shove the paper into the snug pocket of her old jeans. It just about came out again when she tugged her hand out. She rubbed her knuckles. If Uncle Pierre's six kids brought home papers like that, he'd start the fire with them!

And he'd probably take his power saw to the tangle of bare branches in front of her, so tall and thick that not even a glimpse of the peeling green clapboard of Lorraine's house could be seen from the street. Melanie picked an opening in the jungle and scuffed towards the house, kicking up crumbling concrete and rotted leaves.

She forgot about the loose board on Lorraine's step and stopped herself from falling as it suddenly shifted under her weight. Before she could even say a bad word the door opened.

Her mother stood in the doorway, crossed arms hugging the bulge of flesh under her long, grey T-shirt. "Where were you, Melanie? When I got back Lorraine said you hadn't come home for lunch. I was worried."

Melanie cut in. "Yeah, you must have been worried if you weren't even here at lunchtime."

"Now you listen here, my girl," Frances retorted. "I went downtown to the training centre to see about going back to school, and I took the wrong bus back." She tugged her shirt down over her broad hips. "I was worried you'd gotten lost."

"You don't need to worry about me," Melanie snorted. "I can take care of myself." She heard her mother expel a long, slow breath, and knew she was getting to her.

"Did you eat anything at all today?"

Keeping her back to her mother, she shook the loose porch railing back and forth. "They gave me lunch at school," she mumbled.

Her mother persisted. "How come? You

knew you were supposed to come here."

Melanie shrugged, knowing it irritated her mom. But she didn't care. Her mother had no business acting so bossy. She wasn't like that at home. *Kōhkom* was the bossy one and *everyone* listened to *her*, even Uncle Pierre!

Then Melanie reached into her pocket, pulled out the supply list and waved it in her mother's face, like a winning hand in a card game. She watched Frances' lips tighten and heard the intake of breath as she looked at it. Her mother reacted just the way Melanie had thought she would.

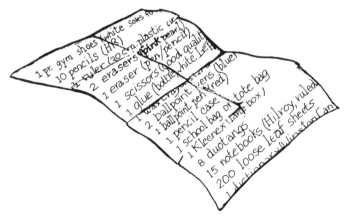

Then why didn't it feel better?

She dragged herself inside after her mother, wrinkling her nose at the stink of stale smoke. Phew. Lorraine was a chain smoker. And Annie, another woman who was staying at Lorraine's with her small daughter while she looked for a place to live, wasn't much better. Even in the porch the odour was strong. This morning she'd smelled it on herself and on her clothes. She made a puking sound. Her mother, hand on the kitchen door, turned and looked at her. Melanie made a face. "It stinks in here," she muttered.

Her mother ignored the comment. Instead she laid the supply list on the table and said, "You still didn't tell me why you didn't come back here for lunch."

Melanie kept her voice low, even though there was no one in the kitchen. "I didn't bother. There's no food here anyway."

Frances put some water in the kettle. "You don't have to whisper," she said. "Lorraine and Annie went to the laundromat and the baby's upstairs sleeping. Lorraine got her cheque today and she's picking up groceries on the way home."

Feeling her mother's eyes on her, Melanie shrugged. She really didn't care.

"How was school?" Frances asked, sitting sideways at the end of the table and tucking one foot behind the other, like *Kōhkom* always did.

A stab of loneliness caught Melanie unawares. Fighting off tears, she struggled with the registration form lodged in the bottom of her pocket and finally plunked it onto the table next to the supply list. "School was fine," she managed in a tight voice.

Frances eyed her over the top of the yellow paper. "I'll do this later," she said, and set it aside, her eyes still intent on Melanie. "Was it awful going there all by yourself?"

"No problem," Melanie lied, smoothing out the paper.

Her mother said nothing. She got up to make her tea. Looking over her shoulder at Melanie, she teased, "Did you show them all how smart you are?"

Melanie ignored the teasing. She chewed the corners of her mouth to stifle anything resembling a smile. Still, she didn't go off to the bedroom and leave her mom alone like she'd intended. She was curious about her mother's day. She hoped it had been as awful as hers.

Without looking at her mom she asked, "Did you get into school?"

Frances set her mug on the table. "I have to go back to see them next Monday."

Melanie said nothing. She'd hoped the answer would be no and her mom would change her mind and they'd go home.

Her mother picked up the supply list but didn't look at it. "My girl," she said, "I can't get you all of this right away. You're going to have to wait."

Melanie shrugged her shoulders. Later, she didn't know what made her say what she said next. She hadn't intended to let her mom off easy. It was probably the dejected look on her mother's face, or the slump of her shoulders that made Melanie feel sorry for her. Before she knew it she was saying, "I don't need all that stuff anyway. Mostly all we use is a pencil and notebook."

She allowed her mom to brush the hair out of her eyes while she stole a sip of tea. She made a face at the strong taste.

"That's what you get for not asking," Frances laughed, pulling Melanie down on her lap and wrapping her soft arms tight around her.

Melanie giggled, giddy with the release of the tension of the past few days. She still felt small when she sat in her mom's arms even though she was only an inch or so shorter than her mom. Frances often teased her that she was as scrawny as a mud hen. And Melanie would retort that her mother was as plump as a Christmas goose! She'd heard that line in a Christmas song and it had stuck in her mind.

She rooted around till she was comfortable. Then she asked, "What if you don't get into school? Can we go back home?"

There was a long silence. Finally, her mother spoke. "No, *nitānis*, we won't be going home for a while … except to visit, like at Christmas."

Melanie stiffened and pushed aside her mom's arms. "Where will you get money then?" her voice taunted as she sprang to her feet.

"The school gives me an allowance. If I can't get in right away I'll find a job somewhere until I'm accepted."

"And what if you can't find a job?" She knew she was pushing again.

Her mother's voice was testy. "Don't worry about it, Melanie. I'll find one."

Not ready to give up, Melanie replied in a light voice, "Better find a good one. I need lots of things for school here." And she leaned close, batting her eyelashes in her mom's face before she turned away.

She gasped when she felt herself being grabbed by the shoulders and half dragged backwards until the backs of her legs touched the chair her mom had been sitting in. She fell onto the seat, struggling to free her arms from Frances' grasp.

Her mom's face loomed over her, placid dark eyes now furious. "You listen to me, my girl. I've had enough of this. You've been acting like a brat ever since we left...."

Melanie wrenched back and forth on the chair but her mother's grip on her arms held. Infuriated by her helplessness, angry tears spilled down her cheeks and she leaned towards her mother and shouted, "I didn't want to come here in the first place! You had no business taking me away from *Kōhkom*!" She sobbed, hiccupping on each word. "And Keena ... and school ... and Elk Crossing!"

Her mother knelt on the floor in front of the chair and slid her hands down Melanie's arms until she cupped Melanie's hands in hers. When she spoke her voice was so quiet, Melanie couldn't help but listen. "Melanie, *Kōhkom* wanted you ..." Her mother faltered, as if searching for the right words. "... she thought it was best for you to come with me too."

Melanie came alive, like a wind-up toy gone berserk. She yanked her hands away from her mother and lunged to her feet. The chair would have fallen over had her mother not caught it. "You're lying!" she stated flatly, legs spread and fists on her hips.

Her mother got to her feet. "Not because she didn't want you…."

Melanie held her ground. "She didn't say it at all!"

Her mother took a sip of tea. "My girl, *Kōhkom* is getting old, you know. She has bad legs, and her blood pressure is high."

Melanie knew about *Kōhkom*'s blood pressure. She was the one who counted out *Kōhkom*'s pills for her every night.

Her mother ran her finger around the rim of her mug. "With the bit of money I made at the store I couldn't support us without *Kōhkom*'s help. And what would we do if *Kōhkom* got sick … or wasn't there any more…."

Melanie bristled at the suggestion that her grandmother wouldn't be around any more. But before she could say anything, her mother went on. "She was glad when I told her I wanted to go back to school and do something with my life." She chuckled. "In fact she said it was about time." Her eyes pleaded with Melanie. "I told her I might have a better chance at sticking it out if you were with me … I wouldn't get so lonely."

Melanie stared at her mother, flabbergasted. "*You* wouldn't get so lonely…!" she sputtered.

Catching her breath, she raged on. "Well, what about me? Did you ever think that I might be lonely? Did you even ask me?"

With that she ripped out of the kitchen and into the squatty little bathroom, slamming the rickety door so hard that the baby upstairs started screaming.

Melanie's Discovery

Melanie pulled her hands up into the sleeves of her jacket, hunched her shoulders against the chilly morning air, and hurried on. The sun was shining, but it was pale and far away and there was no warmth to its rays.

She wore socks today, a pair she'd found in the bottom of the bag that held their clothes. But like the sun, there was no warmth in them either. It had been washed out long ago.

The playground teacher shooed everyone outside to wait for the bell to ring and told the kids they should be wearing warmer jackets in the mornings now.

Melanie huddled against the building. She didn't have a warmer jacket. She'd looked for a sweater to wear under her coat, but she'd left it lying on the floor last evening and Annie's baby had sat on it with a wet diaper. Now she'd have to wait until her mother went to wash clothes at a place that Lorraine called the laundromat.

Finally, the bell rang and the warmth of the hallway stole over her like the heat from the open oven door in *Kōhkom*'s kitchen. It was a while though before Melanie could stop shivering. She kicked off her runners and placed them on an empty shelf away from the others, pushing them as far to the back as she could to hide their raggedy toes.

Her own toes felt as if they were fused together like frozen fillets. She hobbled over to a vent and stood over the heat blowing up through the floor until the surges of pain slackened to throbbing aches.

She tried to hide the hole in her sock underneath her right foot. Nobody seemed to notice. She didn't feel so bad when she saw a few of the other kids had holes in their socks too. They sure didn't seem to care.

When Melanie walked into the room the teacher and some kids were already there. "Melanie," Miss Ryan said, "come, help me move your desk." The teacher walked to a desk sitting against the wall just inside the door.

"We'll put you behind Rachel," she said. "How's that?"

"Good," Melanie replied, gripping the back of the seat. This time she didn't mind when the teacher beamed at her. Miss Ryan seemed a lot nicer than old Miss Critch. The way Miss Critch said your name made you feel like you'd done something wrong. But Miss Ryan said it in a friendly way.

Just before class started, Rachel slipped a notebook onto Melanie's desk. "I have extras," she said, almost in a whisper. "You can have it."

Melanie nodded. "I'll pay you back when I get some," she promised. She'd brought two notebooks today, but at this school you needed a notebook for each subject.

Rachel also let Melanie keep the eraser on her desk and turned around and got it whenever she needed it. That was, until Tanya noticed on her way back from sharpening her pencil. The pink piece of eraser lay in the corner of Melanie's desk.

"You stole my eraser," Tanya hissed at Melanie and picked it up.

Before Melanie had a chance to say a word Rachel swiped it out of her hand. "Tanya, you traded me that eraser last week for a rainbow sticker."

"Yes, but I lost the sticker and I want my eraser back. You had no business giving it to her." Tanya jerked her head in Melanie's direction, but turned the full force of her anger at Rachel.

Rachel's fist was curled tight around the eraser. "It's mine, and I can do what I like with it."

Tanya, her face an angry red, was not about to give up. Her voice rose with each word. "It's mine and I want it back!"

Melanie watched, horrified. Would the teacher blame her? The other kids looked on, enjoying the interruption. Rachel threw the eraser at Tanya. "Here, take your old eraser. We don't want it."

Melanie drew in her breath as the teacher hurried over. "What's the problem?" she asked.

Tanya gestured angrily towards Melanie. "She stole my eraser."

Rachel hurried to explain. "Melanie didn't steal it. Tanya traded it to me last week and I lent it to Melanie."

"Well, I don't want her to have it," Tanya snapped.

"Who has the eraser now?" the teacher asked.

"Tanya does," Rachel replied.

"Give it to me, Tanya." Miss Ryan held out her hand.

Tanya put her hand behind her back. "You'll give it back to her," she accused.

Melanie was shocked. Tanya would never have been allowed to act like that in Miss Critch's class. But Miss Critch was a lot older than Miss Ryan, and meaner.

Miss Ryan sighed and held out her hand. "I'll keep the eraser for now. Please give it to me, or I'll have to phone your mom."

Tanya gave up the eraser and Miss Ryan led her back to her desk. Tanya shrugged the teacher's hand away but Miss Ryan sat her firmly in her desk.

Looking more flustered than annoyed, the teacher stood at the front of the room. Three times she called for quiet before the class settled down, and even then Melanie still heard a few whispers.

She glanced over at Tanya sulking in her desk, frizzy hair covering her face. If she tries to mess with me, Melanie thought, I'll…. Before she had a chance to decide what she would do, Rachel slid a note onto her desk.

Melanie sneaked it down to her lap and read:

Don't worry. Tanya's just jealous. She's always mad at someone. I'm not afraid of her.

At noon Melanie watched as Tanya yanked her coat from the hanger. She looked away as Tanya caught her eye, but not before the girl stuck out her tongue. Then Tanya looked at Rachel, who was walking back to her desk with her lunch in her hand. She yelled at Rachel's back, "Aren't you going to eat lunch at the hall with your friend?"

Rachel swung around. "Shut up, Tanya. You don't have a friend to eat lunch anywhere with."

Tanya yanked viciously on the zipper of her jacket. Her green eyes narrowed just the way they had yesterday. But before she could say anything, Miss Ryan came up behind her and planted both hands on her shoulders. "You'd better go home to lunch right this minute," she said, sounding like she was a little tired of Tanya.

"I'm going," Tanya snapped, twisting free of the teacher's grasp.

Melanie watched her swagger out the door, tossing her frizzy head. The way Tanya talked about her eating lunch at the hall sounded like it was the worst insult she could think of. And she knew Tanya had meant it that way.

She turned her back to the stares of the class and pulled on her jacket. The bannock sandwich was still in her pocket. It was all she had left of the lunch her mom had bought at the corner store last night. She'd eaten the little cake on the way to school and the banana at recess.

Rachel had come up beside her. "You can stay and eat with me. I got lots."

Melanie shook her head. "My mom is expecting me … to go … there," she lied, unable to get out the word home.

Rachel nodded. "I'll see you after, then."

Good thing she hadn't told Rachel this morning that she was staying for lunch. She had been going to but something made her change her mind. She walked out the front door but not towards Lorraine's, or the church hall. Instead, she turned right and walked down the block north from the school. She took several turns, paying no attention to where she was going, and never giving a thought to how she would get back. She knew the streets had names but barely glanced at the words on the green pole at the corner. She hadn't bothered to notice the name of Lorraine's street either.

Streets and house numbers had not been a part of her life. In Elk Crossing, *Kōhkom* lived around the bend and Uncle Pierre lived near the store. She could have told anyone where any resident of the Crossing lived without ever using a street name or house number.

On the other hand, she could have memorized Lorraine's address easily if she'd wanted to. But she didn't.

She reached into her pocket and pulled out the piece of bannock. She walked past some houses and on towards a field. There were dogs barking in the yards but she wasn't scared. There were lots of dogs roaming around in Elk Crossing.

Then at the edge of the field, she thought she saw water. She ran toward it, her heart thumping in time with her steps. Melanie hadn't even realized how much she'd missed the river, until now.

At home, just about every day she'd found time, even if it was for just a few minutes, to run through the narrow path behind *Kōhkom*'s house and climb the big rock, from which she had a perfect view of the river. She'd found toeholds in the rock a long time ago and had no trouble at all hoisting herself up. Lots of the kids could hardly get up at all, unless someone gave them a boost from behind.

But Melanie had liked it best when she went to the river alone. Perched on her rock and gazing across the wide band of water, or letting her eyes drift with the current as far as she could see, Melanie felt little bubbles of joy rise inside her, as light and airy as the froth that the rock skimmed from the river and snuggled close to its base like a lacy collar.

She also loved the rough feel of the rock's solid surface; she even loved its all-over greyness, like a soft shadow easing her eyes from the glare of sun on water.

Now, cutting through some low bushes, Melanie burst out onto the bank of a river. She felt her breath quicken at the sight before her and stood there for a long time. Then she sank down on the bank and let her legs dangle over the edge. The embankment was quite high and there were narrow paths leading down the steep slope to the water's edge, made by animals perhaps, or kids exploring.

She didn't attempt to go down. Sitting on the bank, her eyes surveyed every intriguing twist and turn until the sights and sensations filled her, body and soul, and there was only the river.

She was home again, as safe and secure as if *Kōhkom*'s arms were tight around her. Hugging her knees close to her chest, Melanie rocked back and forth. Lifting her face to the sun, she took a long, deep breath and felt as calm and tranquil as the steady current slipping by her.

The autumn sun, unusually warm, played over her face and she smiled, just because it felt so good. Melanie looked towards the middle of the river. There on a sandbar Canada geese, mallard ducks, and even some gulls strolled about. They seemed to be putting off for a cooler day any thoughts of winter's chill.

She wondered if the geese and ducks on the lake back home had gone south yet. Maybe some of them were taking a rest here before their long journey. She wondered if, on their trip south, they missed the North like she did. She was sure they must.

Then it hit her. She almost slipped down the bank at the thought. She looked at the birds on the sandbar in amazement. Could these be the same ducks and geese that swam on the river back home? Was this the same river? In her excitement, her thoughts tumbled over themselves.

Kōhkom had told her that in the old days

*Mosō*m used to canoe on an overnight trip down the river to Nipawin. And they had passed Nipawin on their way here. She had to find out! She craned her head to see around the bend and had to grab a handful of grasses to keep from falling over the edge.

How could she find out for sure? Maybe Rachel would know, or her mom…. But she didn't think she could wait till she got home this evening. There must be a map of Saskatchewan somewhere in the classroom. She'd ask Rachel to help her find one. Right away.

With a long look, she fixed the river in her mind and stood up to return to school, stopping every so often as she crossed the field to see if she could still catch a glimpse of the water.

Melanie decided this would be her special place in the city, just like the big rock by the river was her special place back home.

Almost stealthily she opened the school's heavy door and walked as softly as she could down the hallway toward her classroom.

"Melanie!" boomed a deep voice from the end of the hallway.

Melanie jumped.

"We've been looking for you," Mr. Mooney said. "Did you know you're not supposed to leave the school ground, unless you're going home to lunch?"

He didn't sound angry, she thought. Actually, he sounded worried.

Still talking, he strode toward her. "I checked Lorraine's house but there was no one at home. I couldn't think where you might have gone."

Melanie was glad her mother hadn't been at home. She'd be in trouble for sure. And she wasn't about to tell Mr. Mooney about the river. He might forbid her to go there. She thought fast. "I went for a walk and I forgot about the time." That was no lie.

"Why didn't you eat at the hall?" Mr. Mooney asked, coming up to her, his hands stuffed in his pockets.

Melanie edged away as he leaned down to look in her face. She said nothing. After Tanya's comments, she knew why she hadn't gone there. But she didn't want to tell the principal that.

"Are you hungry? Would you like some lunch?" Mr. Mooney asked.

Melanie shook her head. He was going to have a sore back if he didn't straighten up. She brushed past him and walked into the classroom.

Now everyone would stare again. Melanie lifted

her head and walked to her desk. Well, let them.

But her classmates were reading their books and Melanie entered the room so quietly most of them didn't even look up. As Melanie seated herself she saw Mr. Mooney crook his finger to the teacher, and Miss Ryan went to the door and whispered with him.

Rachel turned around before Melanie had a chance to nudge her. "Where were you? I waited and waited for you."

"I'll tell you later … I need a map of Saskatchewan."

"What for?"

"I'll tell you later. Is there one here in the room?"

Rachel nodded. "I'll get you one … just a minute." She walked over to a bookshelf on the other side of the room and after a few minutes returned with an atlas of Canada. "There's one in here," she said. "Now what do you want it for?"

But Miss Ryan had returned to her desk and gave them a look that told them to start reading. Rachel turned around.

Melanie turned pages until she found Saskatchewan but the map was full of lakes and rivers and she couldn't find Elk Crossing. Only the big cities, like Saskatoon and Regina, were on this map. She nudged Rachel's shoulder. "I need a better map, with just Saskatchewan on it. Can you get one?"

Rachel nodded again. Melanie watched as she went to the teacher's desk and talked in a low voice. Then she went to the shelf, opened a fat brown envelope and pulled out a map. Laying it on Melanie's desk she whispered, "What do you want it for?"

"Thanks." Melanie was already unfolding the huge highway map. She made a face at the noisy crackle of paper. "I'll tell you later," she promised, without taking her eyes off the map.

Absorbed in her search, she missed Miss Ryan's raised eyebrows. Rachel and a few curious onlookers, seeing the teacher leave her desk and circulate around the room, went back to their books.

Miss Ryan stood over Melanie as her finger traced the squiggly line from Prince Albert east to Nipawin and then north. Peering closer at the fine print Melanie jabbed her finger hard on the paper, at a spot that read Dumont Dam. Squinting, she searched the area around the marking. The squiggly line continued north. There it was! Elk Crossing was on the map right next to the very same squiggly line that went all the way from Prince Albert to Nipawin!

"Did you find what you were looking for?" Her teacher bent over the map.

"Is it the same river?" Melanie asked. "From here to here?" Her finger traced the route again.

"Yes, it is," Miss Ryan assured her. "It's the Saskatchewan River."

"The Saskatchewan River. That's a Cree word. *Kōhkom* … uh … my gramma told me," she corrected herself for the teacher's sake. "It means swift flowing water. At home, though, we just call it the river." Then Melanie realized everyone around her was listening. She folded the map.

"Would you like to borrow the map for a while?" the teacher asked, before moving to the front of the class.

"Yes, please," Melanie replied.

"So you went to the river?" Rachel was curious. "How did you find it?"

As the teacher called the class to attention, Melanie sat up straight in her desk. She put on her most solemn face. Looking Rachel straight in the eye, she said in a half whisper, "I'm Cree. A Cree knows these things."

Rachel giggled and turned around.

Melanie tucked the map inside her desk. She

turned her eyes to the teacher, but her mind was far away, following the river. She wondered how long it would take the water that flowed by her today to reach her rock in Elk Crossing.

A Plan and a Problem

Can you come to my house after school?

Melanie sneaked the tiny scrap of paper to her lap. On the bottom she scribbled *yes*. While she waited for the teacher to turn back to the board she folded the note even more times than Rachel had. Then with a poke to Rachel's shoulder she sent the note back.

After school the two girls wasted no time leaving the building. They skirted around the yellow school bus waiting out front for the last stragglers, and wove in and out between cars loading kids all over the place. They ran across the street, barely escaping a truck that had pulled out of nowhere.

"Yikes! That was close!" Melanie said. She had grabbed Rachel's arm when they crossed the street and let go now, brushing her hair out of her eyes with the hand that held her map.

Rachel spotted it. "Melanie, you're not supposed to bring that map home. You'll get in trouble."

"Teacher let me," Melanie replied. "I'll bring it back."

"What do you want it for anyway? How come you went to the river at lunchtime?"

"I don't know. I just went for a walk and I found it. And guess what! It's the same river as the one back home! It's on the map!" She turned to her friend. "Oh, Rachel, we should go there!"

Rachel giggled. "Where? Your home?"

"I wish we could. You'd love it there. And you'd get to meet Keena. She's my best friend." A pang of loneliness wrenched her insides and left her more determined than ever to go back to the river. "But I don't mean Elk Crossing," she said. "I mean the river here."

"I know," Rachel replied. "I've been there lots. Behind our apartment building there's a short-cut. It only takes a few minutes. In the summer we have picnics down there."

"Then why don't we go?"

Rachel stopped and looked at Melanie. "You mean now? You're crazy. It's too cold."

"It wasn't cold there today. It was nice. You should see all the ducks and geese." Melanie could tell Rachel was interested. "What about Saturday?"

"Maybe," Rachel replied. She grabbed Melanie's arm and her voice rose in delight at her idea. "We could bring a lunch and have a little picnic." She stopped in her tracks. "But there's one problem."

"What's that?"

"I doubt Mom will let me go. Some kids almost drowned there last year."

Melanie bit her lip. She had to go. She just had to. "They must have been fooling around," she said. "We won't even go down to the water. We'll just sit on the bank and watch the birds."

"Are you going to tell your mom?" Rachel asked.

Melanie shook her head. "I don't need to. In Elk Crossing I went to the river by myself all the time. There was a shortcut behind *Kōhkom*'s house too." She danced ahead of Rachel, waving her map above her head. Loneliness forgotten, she hopped up and down as she waited for Rachel to catch up. "It'll be our secret, okay?" she said.

"Okay," Rachel agreed. "We'll make plans when we get to my place."

As they turned into the parking lot of Rachel's apartment she felt a twinge of uneasiness. She hadn't said anything to her mom about stopping at Rachel's on the way home. Oh, well. Her mother had forced her to come here. So she couldn't complain if Melanie visited a friend on the way home from school.

Rachel used the key that hung on a string around her neck to let them in. Melanie stuffed her map into her jacket pocket and pulled on the oversized glass door.

Once inside, the girls chucked off their coats and set about making themselves hot chocolate, with water since there wasn't any milk. "Do you want yours warm or cold?" Rachel asked. She let the tap run, jabbing her finger underneath to test the water before filling her mug.

"Warm," Melanie replied, "but I can do it myself."

She waited for Rachel to finish and then took her time adjusting the water to just the right temperature. She let the warm flow play over her fingers and then her hands, forgetting all about Rachel and the hot chocolate until Rachel asked, "What are you doing there?"

Melanie giggled self-consciously, as if she had been caught playing with a baby's toy. "I like the hot water," she said. "Back home we only have cold, unless we heat some on the stove."

Rachel laughed with her. "That's right," she said. "I almost forgot. We didn't have hot water either. When we lived on the reserve, in the winter time we used to have to haul water from the lake."

Melanie's head bobbed up and down. "Us too," she said, beaming her delight. "But now the water truck comes around to the houses." Rachel's shiny black eyes peered up at her over the rim of her mug, reminding Melanie that she hadn't touched her drink. She shuffled from the sink to the table, taking such care not to spill that she walked stiff-legged.

She curled one leg under her and let the other swing back and forth while she licked the rim of the mug, savouring the sweet chocolate taste. She couldn't ever imagine telling someone like Tanya that back home they didn't have running water, at least not hot.

Rachel broke into her thoughts. "Let's plan our trip to the river." Her face lit up. "Guess what we should do!" She bounced up and down on her chair, slopping her drink all over her hand, and the table too. "Good thing it's not really hot," she said, grabbing a cloth off the counter to clean up the mess.

"What were you going to say?" Melanie asked, impatient for her to go on.

Rachel's black eyes danced. "How about if we put a note in a bottle, and throw it into the river?"

"That's a great idea! It's not that far. I'll show you on the map." Melanie tugged the map out of her pocket and straightened it out on the table. "See, there's Prince Albert," she said, pointing at the map, "and there's Elk Crossing."

Melanie sipped her drink while Rachel traced the route from Prince Albert to Elk Crossing. "Do you have a bottle here?" She set her mug down so hard it was she who spilled this time. "It wouldn't have to be a big one. Do you think it would get there before the river freezes?"

Rachel grinned. "Worth a try. We got lots

of bottles in the storage room."

"Let's make up what we want to say in the note," Melanie suggested.

Rachel went to a kitchen drawer and came back with a half sheet of paper. "Okay, what do you want to say?"

Melanie cupped her chin in her hand and stared up at the ceiling. "We'll put the date for sure," she said. "That way we'll know how long it takes to get there. And we'll tell whoever finds this note to take it to Sarah Bluelake. That's my *Kōhkom*'s name," she told Rachel. "And we'll sign both our names."

Rachel giggled. "Nobody will know who I am."

"So, we'll write after your name that you're my friend."

"Okay," Rachel agreed.

Melanie worked on composing the note while Rachel hunted for a bottle. From another room she yelled to Melanie. "We have to find a cork or something to put in it so the water won't seep in."

Melanie continued to write, cross out, and write again until Rachel bounded back to the table with a small glass Coke bottle in one hand, and a hunk of Styrofoam in the other. "Ta-da!" she boomed.

Melanie looked up. "What is that?" She pointed at the chunk of Styrofoam.

"That's to cork the bottle! Neat idea, huh?"

Melanie scrunched up her nose. "Do you think it'll work?"

"Sure," Rachel said. "Besides, it's all we have." She shrugged. "It'll have to do." She looked at Melanie's paper. "How much did you get done?"

"Well, I don't think we should make it too long. Listen. 'To whom it may concern ….'"

"To whom it may concern," Rachel repeated, "Why did you put that there?"

"You use that if you don't know who's gonna read it," Melanie explained.

"Oh," Rachel accepted her explanation. "Go on."

Oct. 13

To whom it may concern,

This bottle travelled all the way from Prince Albert.
Could you please give this note to my granny, Sarah Bluelake, in Elk Crossing and tell her I miss her.

Melanie Bluelake, (her granddaughter)
Rachel Settee, (my friend)

"What if it doesn't reach Elk Crossing? What if someone finds it somewhere else?" Rachel said.

Melanie chewed on the end of the pen. "You're right." She bent her head and wrote on the bottom.

PS. If you are not in Elk Crossing please throw the bottle back in the river again. Thank you.

Melanie showed the paper to Rachel, who nodded and said, "That should be all right."

The buzzer rang then. Rachel jumped. "Quick," she said, "put the bottle in my room. They're home."

Melanie stood up, jamming her paper into her pocket and folding the map any old way at all before she poked it too into her pocket. "Where?" she asked.

Rachel buzzed the door open. A voice said over the speaker. "Come help me, Rachel."

On her way out the door Rachel yelled, "Down the hall, the room with the posters on the wall!"

Melanie ran down the hall. She didn't want Rachel's mom to come in and find her in the bedrooms. She made it back to the kitchen just as Mrs. Settee, carrying a pile of books in her arms along with a bag of groceries, entered the room. Rachel towed the three-year-old twins she called Jonas and Adam, who zeroed in on what was left of the hot chocolate.

Mrs. Settee flopped down on the tired old green sofa, giving Rachel a chance to say, "Mom, this is Melanie."

"*Tānisi*, Melanie." Mrs. Settee held out her hand to shake Melanie's, a custom Melanie hadn't realized she'd missed since leaving Elk Crossing.

She smiled back at Mrs. Settee and returned the handshake. "How did you know I speak Cree?" she asked.

Mrs. Settee pointed with her chin in Rachel's direction. "Rachel told me," she said.

Melanie was pleased Rachel had told her mother about her. She liked Mrs. Settee. She looked almost as young as Rachel, and she wasn't much bigger either.

Melanie and Mrs. Settee chatted in Cree, while Rachel mixed the boys hot chocolate. Melanie was just about to say she had better go home when Mrs. Settee pleaded with Rachel, "Please, take them to the playground for a half hour while I start supper."

"Come on," said Melanie. "I'll help you."

What could her mom do? Ground her from school? Send her back home? Good idea. She'd have to work on it.

Latching onto the twins' hands, the girls were dragged up the steps and across the parking lot to the swings.

At the end of the half hour Melanie and Rachel were ready to go inside. However, the boys were not and it required a tug-of-war to get them inside the heavy door leading downstairs to the basement.

By this time it was six o'clock and Melanie knew she really should go home. But when Rachel asked her mom if Melanie could stay for supper, Mrs. Settee said, "Sure, as long as her mom knows where she is."

"It's okay," Melanie insisted. "My mom's not home this evening. She's out looking at places for us to live. She won't mind if I stay a bit longer." She didn't want to leave. She liked Rachel's family. For the first time since she'd left *Kōhkom*'s, she felt at home.

When they finished eating, the girls cleaned off the table and dried the dishes while Mrs. Settee washed. Melanie felt good, like when she did the dishes at home with *Kōhkom*. As they talked Mrs. Settee asked, "Where do you live, Melanie?"

"We're staying at a friend of my mom's. Her name is Lorraine. My mom is looking for her own place."

"What street is Lorraine's house on?" Mrs. Settee wanted to know.

"I don't know the street name, but I know where it is," Melanie told her.

"Well, maybe you'd better phone your mother and tell her I'll drive you home in an hour."

Melanie passed Rachel a plate to put up in the cupboard. "Lorraine doesn't have a phone."

"Did you give her our address?" Mrs. Settee asked. "She might be worried. It's getting late."

Melanie shook her head. She was beginning to feel uncomfortable.

Mrs. Settee said, "We'd better take you home right away. It'll just take me a minute to finish up here." Soon they bundled into the aging station wagon, the boys in the front and the girls in the back. "I'll get in first," Rachel told Melanie. "The other door doesn't open from the inside."

The old engine coughed and sputtered but after a few tries it started and they rolled down the street. Melanie peered out the side window. "Turn this way," she instructed Rachel's mother, calling out over the fuss the boys were creating in the front. "You have to turn down there." She kept her eyes peeled for Lorraine's front yard jungle.

But as they turned the corner and drove down the street, they passed her mother on the side-walk. Melanie ducked her head behind the boys' headrest. She sucked in her breath. If her mother was walking around looking for her, she must be in big trouble. Leaning towards the front she made an effort to talk in her normal voice. "See, that's it with all the trees in front."

"You mean the tall hedge there?" Mrs. Settee said, pulling off to the side.

Melanie's seatbelt snapped back. Her hand was already on the door handle. "That's it," she said. "Thanks. Goodnight." She was out of the vehicle almost before it had come to a stop at the curb.

Without looking up the street she ran into the yard and bounded up the steps two at a time, skipping the loose board completely. If she could make it inside before her mother saw her, then maybe she could say she'd been home for a while.

"*Melanie!*"

She stopped in her tracks. Too late. Her mother's moccasins scuffed roughly on the walk behind her. Melanie turned to face her.

Already on the bottom step, her mother clutched her by the shoulders. "Melanie, it's been dark for over an hour. Where did you go? Who were those people?"

Melanie blurted out, "I went to Rachel's house after school …then her mom asked us to take the boys to the park … and then they asked me to stay to supper…."

Her mother sighed and shook her head. "Melanie, what am I going to do with you?" She sank down on the step and pulled Melanie down next to her. She spoke in Cree. Whenever she was mad she spoke Cree. *You don't seem to understand, my girl. This is a city and you can't go roaming around wherever you like until all hours.*

Melanie fumed. "I wasn't roaming around. I was at Rachel's, I told you."

It was as if she hadn't spoken. Her mother appeared to have no intention of listening.

"Melanie," she said, "from now on, you come straight home after school. Do you understand that?"

Melanie pulled away from her mother's grasp. "No, I don't understand!" she yelled. She couldn't stop the tears from spilling down her cheeks. First the principal had told her she couldn't leave the school grounds. Now her mother wouldn't allow her to visit her friend, the only friend she had in the city. "Why should I come here? It's not my home. Why don't you send me back to *Kōhkom*? At least I can go to the river there, and I can go visit my friends."

"What does the river have to do with this?" A puzzled frown wrinkled her mother's brow. She smoothed back hair already caught tight with an elastic band at the nape of her neck. She always did that when she was trying to figure something out.

Infuriated, Melanie jumped up. "Never mind." She spat out the words. Her mother didn't know anything about her, not a thing. She rubbed her eyes, trying to wipe the tears away. "What do you care?" she muttered and left her mother standing on the porch.

She stomped straight to the bedroom and threw herself on the lumpy mattress, hiding her face in the pillow until long after it was wet with tears and sniffles.

At last her sobs subsided to uneven breaths. She realized she was chilly and quickly got ready for bed, not wanting to be up when her mother came into the room. Before falling asleep she moved right in by the wall. Tonight she wanted to be as far away from her mother as she could get. The map she clutched in her hand, but there was no way she was ever going to tell her mom about it or the river now.

Melanie woke in the morning with the map under her cheek. She lay stiff against the wall until she felt the mattress give and knew that her mother sat on the edge of the bed.

"*Waniskā*, Melanie." Her mother reached over and shook her shoulder.

Melanie shrank from her touch. "There's no school," she said, pulling the blankets over her head.

"No school?" her mother echoed. "Are you sure? How come?"

In a huff Melanie threw off the covers, sat up, and grabbed for her jeans at the foot of the bed. She yanked a paper out of a pocket and tossed it on the bed. "Today is interview day," she said, as if explaining something to a young child. "The other kids got their report cards yesterday. I didn't get one because I just started school here. But the teacher wants to see you anyway. The time is on the paper."

Her mother picked up the sheet and looked at it. She had that anxious look on her face again. Melanie knew it meant her mother wasn't going to meet the teacher. Fully awake now she got out of bed. "Why won't you go?" she asked. "Miss Ryan is nice. She just wants to meet you."

Her mother didn't look at her. She pulled the covers up over the bed, fluffed the pillows, and said nothing.

But Melanie wanted an answer and kept asking while Frances straightened and tidied everything in the cramped room that could be straightened and tidied. Finally, in her unhurried manner, her mother said, "No, I'll go another time …" She paused and Melanie noticed the worried crease in her forehead. "… when things are better." Then, without looking at Melanie, she left the room.

Melanie sat on the edge of the bed, tears stinging her eyes. Everyone else's mother would go and she would be the only one whose mom wouldn't be there. And the teacher would ask her all kinds of questions. And probably Tanya would bug her about it.

She hadn't noticed her mother coming back into the room. Not until she spoke. "Melanie, if it means that much to you, I'll go."

Melanie rubbed the back of her hand across her eyes. "Why don't you want to go anyway?"

The bed creaked and sagged as her mother

sat down next to her. She didn't say anything at all for a while. Melanie watched her smoothing out wrinkles in the blanket. When the last wrinkle was gone she sighed. Then she said, "I don't want to go because I can't afford to get your supplies yet. And I don't know what to say if she asks me about it. And then she'll probably ask me if I found a place to live yet. And I'll have to say no to that too. And I haven't started school."

Melanie heard the tremor in her mother's voice. She didn't know what to say or do. Her insides felt numb.

Her mother went on. "I guess I'm not doing a very good job of looking after you, am I?" She put her arm around Melanie and laid her chin on Melanie's head. "With *Kōhkom* everything was always taken care of. I never even thought much about it. I never realized…."

Just then Annie poked her head around the door and asked if Frances could help move the baby's crib away from the dresser. Melanie was left wondering what her mother had been going to say.

Now she felt bad about saying all those things last night. Even though they were true.

First thing the next morning Miss Ryan greeted Melanie with her big smile. "I'm sorry I didn't get to meet your mom yesterday," she said. Her tone was apologetic, as if somehow it were her fault.

Melanie calmly lied, "She wasn't feeling well."

At hometime the teacher gave her another note with a new interview time.

Once out the door Melanie ripped it into a trillion tiny pieces. For the first time since leaving home her heart felt light, as light as the papers fluttering in the breeze.

The River

Saturday!

Melanie's feet pounded the concrete as she ran down Fifteenth Street. Though she and Rachel were still a block apart they spotted each other at the same time and waved their arms wildly in the air.

"Did you bring the bottle?" Melanie cupped her hands to her mouth and yelled to Rachel. But her friend was still too far away to hear.

Breathless, Melanie slowed to a walk and, hands still to her mouth, blew on them to warm them. The cold was sharp even though it was already an hour past noon and the sun was out. Melanie checked the sky. She hoped it wouldn't snow, at least not until they got back from the river. The sun looked like its battery was weak.

A pitiful pinpoint of light struggled to break through the overcast sky.

With Rachel only a half block away, Melanie broke into a run again. The two girls collided, laughing in the excitement of their Saturday secret. "Watch out, you'll break the bottle!" Rachel patted her jacket.

"Where is it?" Melanie couldn't see a pocket. "Whose jacket are you wearing anyway?"

"My mom's old one. See, it fits me!" Rachel twirled around for Melanie to inspect. "And it's even got a pocket inside!" She unzipped it halfway to show the bottle, its neck sticking out of a deep plaid-lined pouch.

"Neat!" Melanie replied. "I'd like to hold it! But it's safer in there."

"You get to throw it in the river," Rachel said, zipping up her jacket.

The girls headed back in the direction Rachel had come from. "We have to walk down the alley behind my apartment building. There's a path. That's the fastest way, and the easiest one too. Hardly any bushes."

"Okay," Melanie agreed. "Did you bring anything to eat?"

Rachel patted her right pocket. "Some cookies and two chocolate bars, one for you and one for me. Do you like Snackaroos?"

"Mm-mm-mm!" Melanie rolled her eyes. "I have two pieces of fried raisin bannock and some bubblegum. Do you want a piece of gum now?" She dug her hand into a bulging pocket.

"Okay." Rachel held out her hand.

Melanie squeezed two gumballs out of a plastic wrapper. "What colour do you want?"

Rachel chose the red one and popped it into her mouth while Melanie took the yellow one. They reached the alley and walked past the apartments, collars turned up around their ears and hands jammed into their pockets against the bitter wind. "I hope the river's not frozen yet," Rachel said, turning around to walk with her back to the wind.

Melanie did the same. "It won't be. I was there just a few days ago and there wasn't a sign of any ice." Melanie sniffed loudly. The chill was making her nose run.

"Yeah, but the temperature's been below freezing every day this week. And the nights have been really cold. I asked Mom if she thought there'd be ice on the river yet and she said she wouldn't be surprised if there was."

Melanie stopped in her tracks and looked at Rachel, her eyes wide with dismay. "You told your mom?"

"No, silly. I just asked…."

"But what if she figures it out?"

"Why would she? I never said anything about going there and we'll be back in an hour or so."

"I hope there's nobody else there."

"I doubt it," Rachel said, poking Melanie in the ribs. "Who else but you would be crazy enough to want to go there when it's as cold as this?" she said, tugging the hood of her jacket up over her head as she turned back into the wind.

Melanie punched her friend's arm. "Well, you're going so you must be crazy too." She took off at a run, her braid flying out behind her like the tail of a kite. She looked over her shoulder at Rachel chasing after her with a lopsided gait, her right hand holding the bottle in her pocket.

They ran past the last house and across the

open field, the ground hard as concrete under their feet. Running into low bushes flanking the river, Melanie heard them snap and crack in the cold as Rachel followed close behind.

Melanie stopped in the midst of the bushes, awed all over again by the broad band of water before her. It must be almost as wide as the school playground, she figured, wider than the river back home for sure. At least the part she could see was.

Winter had come to the river too. The fall browns and beiges of sandbars and banks and bare trees were all but gone today. The river was an ashen grey and a frosty fog hung over the water, stretching right to the chalky white shoreline just ahead.

"It's like a different world," Melanie marvelled.

Rachel had come up behind her. "The spot where you were is probably closer to the school," she said, kicking aside a twig that had fallen across her foot. "We can walk down that way, if you like."

Melanie didn't reply. She just wanted to look and look.

"See those two big patches of ice?" Rachel asked, pointing past Melanie. She shoved her hand back into her pocket. "I wonder if the bottle will make it. Maybe we should wait till spring?"

With a shake of her head forceful enough to flick her long heavy braid over her shoulder, Melanie replied, "Not a chance. We're going to throw it in now. Let's find a clear space where the water is flowing really fast."

Rachel took the lead as they followed the narrow footpath around the bend. Melanie tracked close behind her, her eyes sweeping the river in search of more of the blobs of ice Rachel's mom had said there might be. And there they were, three of them, three more chances that their bottle might not make it. Melanie scowled at the congealed masses as if she could dissolve them by sheer willpower.

"Let's walk along the bank and see if we can find a stretch where there's no ice at all," Rachel suggested.

"Good idea." As she walked, Melanie scanned the river steadily until she just about tripped on a root sticking right out in the middle of the narrow footpath. The path turned away from the river then, through some higher bush, and wound back along the wide curve of the high bank again. Melanie groaned. "There's even more ice here."

Rachel stopped, so suddenly that Melanie bumped into her. She put her finger to her mouth to caution Melanie to be quiet and then pointed down over the high bank.

Melanie looked down. Her eyes widened, and within seconds her mouth did too, into a broad smile. She couldn't believe their good fortune. There, on a sizable stretch of ice sheltered by a crook in the river, sat a Canada goose.

The girls sank to their knees and watched, as still as stumps of deadwood. The goose, unperturbed, continued to gaze downriver. Melanie searched the sky, but could neither see nor hear any sign of more. She wondered what this goose was doing there on the river all alone. The geese around Elk Crossing had left just before she did.

She wondered if this goose had been one of them. It looked lonely there on the ice all by itself, staring downstream as if it missed something, or some place. Maybe it was lonely for the North too. It could even be stranded here all by itself without friends or family. If she could only get closer she'd rub that sleek, black head and stroke its white cheeks, and whisper that she knew what it felt like to be all alone and lonely in a strange place.

Rachel edged closer to her. "He's not moving," she whispered. "Do you think he's hurt?"

Melanie put her finger to her lips and shrugged. "I don't think so," she whispered. "I can't see any blood. The wings look like they're okay."

"Should we make a noise, and see if it flies away?"

Melanie shook her head. She didn't want it to leave, not yet. "It might be stuck in the ice and if we made a noise it would really be scared." She couldn't bear the thought of frightening the beautiful creature. She beckoned to Rachel to move back.

They edged away from the bank until they could only see the goose by craning their necks.

"One time Uncle Pierre found a goose stuck in ice," Melanie whispered, "and he had to crawl up close and chop it free. He told me how scared it was. Its wings were very powerful and it tried to beat at Uncle. But when he got it free it dragged itself a few feet away from him and then it turned around and bowed its head low and beat its wings once before it took flight. Uncle told me the goose was telling him *ki nanāskomitin*."

"Do you think this goose is stuck?"

"It might be," Melanie replied. "We have to get closer and find out."

"We don't want to scare it."

"Let's go back a bit and find a way down to the water." Melanie turned. The raw wind in her face made her eyes water.

Rachel caught her sleeve. "Melanie, that bank is as high as a house. We'll never be able to get down there. It's too dangerous."

Melanie pulled away, but Rachel held on. There was a quiver to her whisper. "Melanie, something might happen."

Melanie turned on her. "What if that bird is stuck? Do you want to leave it here to die?"

"No, but…."

"Then, come on." Melanie held Rachel's arm. Her fingers were purple, and numb.

They scrambled back around the bend and sat at the top of the bank looking over the edge. It was a long way down.

"Oh, Melanie," Rachel whimpered. "I'm scared to go down there."

Melanie, shivering, blew on her hands and tucked them under her armpits. She leaned over for a better look. "It's not too bad," she reassured Rachel. "See, there's a path going down. I'll go first and you come behind me." She looked at

Rachel then. "If you're scared, you can wait here for me."

Rachel looked as if she were about to cry, but shook her head. "If you go, I'm going too." Melanie heard the quiver in her voice.

Melanie edged forward until one foot and then both were on the narrow trail. She inched ahead and waited for Rachel. Then on their behinds they slipped and slid, every now and then grabbing at stumps and sticks and dead weeds to keep their balance. "It's not as bad as I thought it would be," puffed Rachel as they neared the bottom. "Be careful, Melanie," she cautioned. The river came right to the edge of the steep bank.

Melanie clambered over the rocks at the edge of the water. They were wet and slippery. She gasped as the icy water seeped in through the toes of her runners. After, she didn't bother to stay dry. She was so cold already, a bit more didn't seem to make much difference.

"My toes are wet," Rachel muttered, as they rounded the bend.

The goose was so close Melanie felt she could almost reach out and touch it. Still it gazed downstream, not even ruffling a feather.

"Now what?" Rachel asked as they stood and watched it.

Melanie said nothing.

"Let's yell and wave," Rachel whispered.

"Are you crazy?" Melanie whispered back. "We'll scare it half to death if it can't fly away."

"Well then, what can we do?" Rachel asked.

"I'm going out there."

"You can't. The ice is too thin. You'll break through."

"Not if it's been freezing every night this week."

"Melanie, you can't go out there. Look, there's still water at the edge."

"It's always like that, even at home. That's nothing to worry about. I'll lie down and crawl out."

"Melanie, no!" Rachel grabbed at her but Melanie shrugged her hand away. Sounding desperate, Rachel pleaded, "I'll never come here with you again. You said we wouldn't even come down to the water."

"Yes, but we didn't know about the goose then. We just can't let it freeze to death, Rachel."

"We'll phone someone to come and get it." Rachel's chin quivered. "I'm scared, Melanie. What if you drown?"

"I won't drown. I know what to do. Besides, it's not deep enough there." Melanie handed Rachel the food from her pocket. Then, without bending her legs, she doubled over and placed her bare hands on the ice past the strip of open water at the edge. The ice held.

Rachel pulled off the scarf she wore tucked inside her jacket. "Here, hold this so I can pull you back if...." Her quavery voice stopped in mid-sentence.

Melanie turned her head, grabbed the end of the scarf, and tucked it under her left hand. Gingerly she placed her right knee onto the ice and slid one hand ahead of her and then the other, testing the surface. Then she flattened out on her stomach.

The goose was only about a metre away. Melanie let go of Rachel's scarf and stopped to tug her sleeves down over her hands, already splotched purple and red with cold. She wiggled forward on her forearms, the only sound the slow scrape of her jacket on the ice – except for Rachel's pitiful bleating, "Careful Mel, careful...."

Melanie shuffled closer, her eyes locked on the goose. It didn't move. Another shuffle. If she stretched out her hand she could just about touch the bird. But she'd have to get closer if she wanted to help it.

However, before she could draw a breath, the goose spread its great wings. Melanie stopped in mid-creep. Her tense body twitched in fright. The wings beat the air, practically in her face. She could feel the wind they created. Her heart fluttered as fast and hard as the goose flapped. She gulped a mouthful of icy air. Before she could make soothing noises to calm the frightened creature, it took to the air. She heard herself utter a strangled cry.

From shore Rachel squealed, "Hurry Melanie, get back here quick!"

But it was already too late. The air around Melanie's head crackled with a racket like reverberating rifle shots.

Melanie froze. Paralyzed by an overpowering fear, she stared at the huge crack that appeared under her hands. She watched it splinter into a thousand tributaries all around her.

It must have been her own cry of terror that triggered her to act, or maybe it was Rachel screaming her name. On hands and knees, Melanie whipped around and struck out for shore, in her panic, slithering right by Rachel's scarf stretched out on the ice.

She felt her hands touch the icy water at the edge of the river. Then she was knee deep in it, and Rachel was reaching out to her and crying. "We have to get home right away!" she blubbered.

On hands and knees they clawed their way up the steep embankment. This time Rachel led the way. Melanie scrambled behind her, wincing at the pain in her feet and hands. About halfway up, Rachel, turning around to check on her, sobbed, "Oh, Melanie, you're bleeding."

She looked at the scrape on her hand. Blood mixed with dirt and torn skin. She pulled her sleeve down over it and crawled on, gritting her teeth. Her knee hurt too where her old jeans had given out. It was probably bleeding too. She didn't take the time to look.

At last they reached the top and stumbled across the field. Melanie felt like she was walking on stumps. "Are your feet numb too?" she asked Rachel, through chattering teeth.

Rachel nodded. "Here, lean on me," she said. "We're almost there now." They turned up the path away from the river. Melanie had never been so cold in her life.

She stopped and removed her reddened hands from her pockets and stuck them under her armpits, in an attempt to ease the terrible pains in her fingers.

"Here, put your hand in my pocket," Rachel said. Melanie eased her left hand into the warm lining, and Rachel cupped her own hand around it. She closed her eyes to shut out the pain. It did no good. She shivered, chilled to the bone.

With Melanie leaning on Rachel, they hobbled along the back alley and into the apartment building. "Is your mom home?" Melanie asked, afraid to hear Rachel's answer.

"I don't think so," Rachel replied. There was an apprehensive look on her face. "She was going to take the boys shopping for winter boots."

They let themselves into the apartment, hardly daring to breathe, and waited in the doorway listening. The apartment was quiet.

Rachel pushed the door shut. "Quick," she said, "go into the bathroom and take off your socks and jeans. I'll get you some dry ones."

Melanie did as she was told. In a minute Rachel came in. She laid the dry clothes down and set about running the tub, not saying a word until she had adjusted the water. "Sit on the edge of the tub and put your feet in," she told Melanie. "The water's lukewarm; it won't burn you." She looked at Melanie, an anxious look on her face.

"Are your feet still numb?"

"They're starting to feel better now," Melanie lied. She eased her feet into the water, and rubbed them gently with her hands, shutting her eyes tight. When she opened them, Rachel was still there, her face as pinched as Melanie's toes.

"How do they feel now?" Rachel asked.

Melanie grimaced. "Well, at first my toes felt like someone was hitting them with a hammer. Now they just feel like someone's sticking pins in them. I think that's better, don't you?" She cocked her head sideways and looked at Rachel.

Rachel giggled nervously. "I'll make some hot chocolate while you change." She handed Melanie some socks and pants. "You'll have to wear my mom's pants. Mine are too small for you. I'll put your stuff in the dryer."

While Rachel jacked up the thermostat Melanie curled up in a shivering ball on the chesterfield. She tucked a cushion around her feet. Then with a scalding cup of hot chocolate clutched in a still splotchy hand, she felt almost alive again.

Rachel settled herself next to Melanie. Her face was pale and her eyes, under her bangs, were dark and solemn. She stirred the top of her drink with her finger a few times before she spoke. "You know, we were really lucky…."

"Speak for yourself," Melanie said, a ghost of a grin on her face, "I almost froze to death."

A wan smile touched Rachel's purplish lips. "I thought I'd die I was so scared…."

Melanie set her mug on the floor and clamped her hand on Rachel's shoulder. "Listen here," she said, in mock indignation, "I was the one who had reason to be scared. That ice wasn't cracking into smithereens under your skinny little body."

Rachel giggled in spite of herself and tried to wrestle Melanie down on the sofa. "It's all your fault," she said, grabbing the cushion off Melanie's feet and slapping at her with it.

Melanie slid to the floor. "No, it isn't," she said, a triumphant look on her face. "Whose bright idea was it in the first place to throw the bottle in the river?"

Rachel made a face at her. "Well, you didn't have to listen."

Then Melanie remembered. "Rachel, we didn't throw it in. Where is it?"

Rachel lifted her jacket off the chair where she'd tossed it and pulled the bottle out of the pocket.

"We'll have to go back," Melanie said.

Rachel lifted the bottle as if to hit her. "You know, you're insane! You could have drowned. I should hit you with this."

"Can I have it then?"

"No, you can't. It's staying in my room until spring. Maybe then —just maybe —we'll go back."

"Well, at least the goose is okay."

"What do you mean okay? It was okay all along."

"Well, at least now we know it's okay."

"I wish I could say the same for you. I think that bird has more sense than you do." Rachel plunked the bottle down on the table. When Melanie reached for it, she said, "Oh no, you don't. I'm putting this away."

Rachel went to put the bottle in her bedroom. Melanie, chin in hand, stared into her hot chocolate as she stirred it. She wished they been able to throw the bottle in.

"Guess what we still have!" Rachel whizzed by her and dropped both their bags of treats onto the table. "How about some chocolate with your chocolate?" she laughed, pushing a Snackaroo in front of Melanie.

However, her laugh died quickly when they heard a key turn in the apartment door.

The Move

*M*elanie marched down the street, clutching a brown paper bag close to her. It had taken her four days to convince Rachel to let her keep the bottle. She'd had to promise that she wouldn't even think of going to the river again by herself.

Melanie didn't mind. After last weekend she was content to let things be for a while, but only as far as the bottle was concerned. She and Rachel had gotten into a lot of trouble. Rachel was grounded for a whole week and after Mrs. Settee talked to her mother Melanie was grounded too. Of course, her mother blamed it all on her and wouldn't even listen when Melanie tried to tell her about the poor goose on the ice.

Melanie was sure of one thing, though. As

soon as she could find a way, she was going home. Away from Lorraine's stinky house, and away from her bossy mother.

Melanie turned into Lorraine's front yard to see her mother in the window, beckoning to her. She scowled, wondering what she'd done this time. She couldn't think of anything. She shifted the bottle to her other arm and opened the kitchen door to see their bag packed and leaning against the wall. Before she could ask where they were going, Frances said, "We're moving...."

Melanie laid the bottle on the counter. "Where?" She held her breath, sensing that this was not good news.

Frances' stubby fingers fumbled with the zipper of her purse. Still tugging at it, she replied, "We're going to stay with a friend, Victoria, for a while. It's harder than I thought to find a place to rent and we've stayed with Lorraine long enough." She smoothed back her hair, an anxious gesture, and looked at Melanie. "I think you'll like it at Victoria's."

"Sure," Melanie sneered. "That's what you said about moving to Prince Albert too." She slouched against the counter and clicked her fingers against a dirty glass. The sullen look on her face was meant to let her mother know exactly how she felt about this idea.

"Stop that, Melanie, you'll break the glass." Her mother sank heavily onto a chrome chair. She picked a woolly knob, and then another, off her black sweat pants.

"So, who cares?" Melanie didn't care if she broke a hundred glasses.

"You mind yourself, my girl. You're getting to be too mouthy these days." Her mother's normally mild voice was stern. Melanie knew she would get nowhere by angering her mother. She changed her tone, ready to coax her mom. "Then send me home to *Kōhkom*. Please, Mom. I'll be good there, huh?"

When her mother didn't reply Melanie thought she might have a chance. She pushed a chair closer to her mother and sat down, balancing herself on the edge of the seat and raising the chair's back legs off the canvas floor. "Can I go back home, Mom? Please? Till you find a place?"

But her mom shook her head, slowly, as if she were in pain. "No, Melanie, you belong with me."

Melanie crumpled. She laid her head on the table, letting the chair legs hit the floor with a bang. She wouldn't move again, unless it was to their own place. She had just made a new friend and she wasn't going to start all over.

Her mother leaned toward her. Her voice was tender. "You'll like Victoria," she said. "We used to go to school together back home years ago. I ran into her today at the corner store and she wants us to come and stay with her until we find a house we can rent."

But Melanie refused to be coaxed. She jumped up from the table, her eyes and her voice defiant. "I'm not going. I don't care what you say. I don't want to go to another strange house and I don't want to go to another strange school either." In spite of her brave talk she couldn't stop her chin from trembling.

Relief swept across Frances' face. "Is that what you're thinking? That you'll have to go to another school?" She reached out her hand, but Melanie moved away from her. "You don't have to go to another school, my girl. You can stay where you are. Victoria doesn't live that far from here."

Melanie, leaning against the wall, didn't feel any better. "Why can't we just go home?" she asked, sinking down to the floor. She dug her fists into her eyes, but it didn't help. The tears leaked past and dribbled down her face.

Frances shrugged on the coat that had been

draped over the back of a chair. She shook her head, but didn't speak until the jacket had settled around her. "Melanie, I told you, we're staying in Prince Albert." She paused. "We'll find a place of our own soon - promise."

Liar...! Liar...! Melanie screamed at her mother, but only in her mind. "I don't believe you," she said aloud, emphasizing every word. She kicked out her foot and made contact with the leg of the chair.

Frances looked down at her. "Come say goodbye to Lorraine and Annie."

Melanie kicked again.

"The least you can do is say thank you for letting us stay here."

Another kick.

Frances sighed and went to the living room to say her goodbyes. Her sagging shoulders and her coat collar, turned under so that it bulged on the back of her neck, made her seem as stooped as an old woman.

Alone in the kitchen, Melanie remembered her bottle and stuffed it into the bag just as her mother returned. Then she yanked open the door and waited on the porch until her mom had gone down the walk. In her own good time Melanie followed. She knew she should say goodbye but she wouldn't. That would show her mom!

Lorraine wouldn't care anyway. All she cared about were her cigarettes. She was so busy smoking and watching television she didn't even change the baby for hours. Melanie had seen the baby's diaper rash; it looked sore. She felt nothing about leaving. It was as if she had never stayed in that house at all.

They walked the seven blocks to Victoria's apartment in silence, with Melanie staying well behind her mother.

Her spirits brightened a tiny bit when she realized that they were walking in the same general direction as Rachel's apartment. But she said nothing to her mother. They weren't talking. Even if they were, Melanie wouldn't admit to her mother that there was anything the least bit good about this move.

Frances set the bag down on the sidewalk and waited for her. "You'll like Victoria," she said. Melanie knew her mother was trying to see if she was still mad. She walked past, her shoulders drooping as if she were the one carrying the bag.

Frances talked to Melanie's back. "You'll have to come straight home every day after school. I don't want to cause Victoria any trouble. It's really nice of her to let us stay there."

Melanie silently mimicked her mother.

Frances stopped again. This time she checked the piece of paper that held Victoria's address. "*Ēhē*," she said. "*Ēyako-ōma*." They turned up the walk to Victoria's apartment. Frances rang the buzzer. Melanie was surprised at the Cree voice that came through the intercom. Almost before the voice finished speaking a door banged open and a tall slim woman, with a braid even longer than Melanie's hanging over her shoulder, bounded out to meet them. Victoria led them inside her small first floor apartment.

She made a fuss over Melanie. "Those beautiful eyes!" she exclaimed. "And that hair. We could be twins!" She laughed as she talked and Melanie couldn't help but laugh too. She especially enjoyed Victoria saying, "You don't look a bit like your mom did when she was small. She was short and pudgy, just like she is now!"

Her mother laughed so hard she had to wipe the corners of her eyes with a tissue. "Victoria, you haven't changed a bit," Frances said, shaking her head and laughing some more.

"Well, I hope not!" Victoria retorted as she set the kettle on the burner. "I sure thought about you often over the years, Frances. What have you been doing with yourself?" She winked at Melanie. "I see you've done one worthwhile thing. That's more than I can say!"

Melanie grinned and sipped on the ginger ale Victoria had poured her. She lost interest in the conversation while Victoria and her mother caught up on each other's lives. So she looked around the place, coming back to the table every now and then for another sip of her drink.

The apartment was tiny and had only one bedroom. Melanie figured out that her mom would sleep on the aging floral sofa and she'd sleep on the floor. There was a carpet, so it wouldn't be too hard.

But the best thing was that Victoria had a phone. Melanie had begged *Kōhkom* and her mom to have a phone installed. But *Kōhkom* had been dead set against it and when *Kōhkom* made up her mind about something there was no changing it. Melanie wished she knew Rachel's number. But she felt too shy yet anyway to ask Victoria if she could use the phone.

She couldn't help but like Victoria, though. Maybe she'd given her mother too much of a hard time. When the two adults took their tea and moved to sit on the sofa Melanie went over to sit next to her mom. She leaned against her for a while enjoying the cosy feeling. Then she reached up and gave Frances a peck on the cheek.

Victoria smiled. "Now there's a girl who loves her mom," she said.

"Well, I think she's trying to tell me something. Right, my girl?" Frances put an arm around her.

Melanie nodded and buried her head in her mom's shoulder, embarrassed by the attention.

Frances spoke to Victoria. "It's hard on her, all this moving about."

Victoria nodded. "Yes, it must be." Then to Melanie she said, "We're gonna find you a really nice place to live. Don't you worry."

Melanie said nothing. She was glad Victoria didn't know about the fight she'd had earlier with her mom.

Supper was delicious! Victoria boiled some whitefish her brother had brought her from home and Frances made bannock. They ate it hot from the oven, with butter melting on top. There were even blueberries from Victoria's freezer. Melanie couldn't help but think of suppertime at *Kōhkom*'s. She chewed slowly, her thoughts on *Kōhkom*.

The rest of the evening flew by. Melanie made up her bed on the floor and slept on homemade quilts next to the sofa where her mother was sleeping.

In the morning she assured her mom and Victoria she knew the way to school. She left a bit early, just in case. However, finding her way was a cinch. She searched out Rachel as soon as she reached the schoolyard. "Come here," she said, grabbing her friend's arm and dragging her off the tire swing. "I have to tell you something!"

"I hope it's not about the river!" Rachel giggled. She jumped off and allowed Melanie to drag her away.

Melanie couldn't wait to tell her. "Guess what?" Without waiting for Rachel to reply, she hurried on, "We moved, and I think I might be living closer to you now, because when I came to school this morning I had to come your way for part…."

Rachel cut in. "Where? What's the address?" She jumped up and down, grabbing Melanie's arm.

"I don't know the address, but it's across the tracks and it's not far from the Food Plus store."

"The Food Plus is only a block from me!" Rachel squealed. "I'll walk home with you after school and you can show me, okay? Did your mom find a place to live?"

"No," Melanie said. The words poured out of her. "Victoria is my mom's friend … they used to go to school together … and she has a phone, so I'll be able to call you."

The bell rang then, and Melanie told Rachel all about Victoria as the girls walked into the school arm in arm.

The morning dragged. Even the seconds seemed slow, Melanie thought. Finally, it was recess time and the two girls raced to the swings. As they jumped on Rachel said, "Maybe next week your mom will let you come over to my place, do you think? I won't be grounded any more then."

Before Melanie could reply, Tanya spoke from where she stood at the pole that supported the swing. "How come you're going to Rachel's house after school? You don't live near her," she said, her voice as peevish as a spoiled brat at someone's else's birthday party.

Rachel answered for her. "Now she does. She moved."

Tanya's eyes bored into Melanie. "Did you find a place to live?"

Melanie was tempted to tell her it was none of her business. But she was feeling so happy she decided to be pleasant to Tanya. "No," she replied, working her feet back and forth so she could go higher, "we're staying with my mom's friend."

"Another friend?" scoffed Tanya. "Too bad she can't buy you some pencils and paper." She started to walk away. She didn't get far.

Melanie jumped off the swing and shoved her, sending Tanya sprawling on the frozen ground. Tanya lay there open-mouthed, with bits of loose gravel imprinted in her hands and knees. Then with a squeal she jumped to her feet and charged at Melanie, her fingernail catching the side of Melanie's chin. Melanie caught her by the arms and this time shoved her backwards. Tanya hit the ground again.

The next second the playground was in an uproar. Tanya sat where she had fallen and screamed over and over, "She hit me! She hit me!"

The playground teacher came on the run to see what the fuss was. Puffing from the exertion of running across the playground, she leaned over Tanya and helped her up.

Melanie watched.

The teacher looked from Tanya to Melanie. "What happened here?" she demanded.

Tanya wailed and pointed at Melanie.

Melanie curled her fists and said nothing.

Receiving no reply, the teacher placed her hands on both girls' shoulders. "Let's go see the principal."

Tanya snivelled all the way to the office. Melanie felt like gagging her.

Mr. Mooney raised his eyebrows upon seeing the girls. He crossed his arms and stood in front of them. "Well, what's this all about?" he asked.

Tanya blubbered, "Melanie … Melanie…."

Melanie stood there like a stick of deadwood.

"Tanya, you go clean up and then come back here," Mr. Mooney ordered.

He turned to Melanie. "Tell me your side of the story, Melanie." When she said nothing, he asked, "Would you like to write down what happened?" Melanie stared at the floor, her long bangs covering her eyes. She sniffed.

The principal's tone softened. "I can't help you if you won't tell me what happened," he said.

Tanya returned then, sniffling, her hands held gingerly in front of her. Melanie looked at her in disgust. The principal was out of luck if he thought that she was going to apologize to that whining big mouth. She'd bet that Miss Mouth would leave her alone in the future.

Mr. Mooney sat on the corner of his desk.

"Well, Tanya, are you ready to tell me what happened?"

Through the sniffles and hiccups Tanya blamed Melanie for everything. "It's all her fault. I didn't touch her. She pushed me down."

Mr. Mooney shifted his position. Melanie could feel his eyes intent on her. "Is that so, Melanie? Is that how it happened?"

His question raised nothing but a look of scorn from Melanie. She was not about to tattle her business with Tanya to the principal.

Mr. Mooney stood up. "While I check into this further, you girls can write up what happened. Tanya, you sit here." He pulled out the secretary's chair. "Melanie, you sit in here." He pointed to the chair by his desk, the one she'd used when she'd registered. Then he closed the office door and left.

When he returned he took their papers. Melanie had scrawled, *I pushed her.* When Mr. Mooney asked why, she shrugged her shoulders and flicked her braid around to her back.

"I asked around," said the principal, "and it seems Tanya had something to do with this as well." He paused. "But you're not going to tell me about it, are you?" Another pause. Then Mr. Mooney said, "I want you and Tanya to stay away from each other for a while."

You better tell her that, Melanie felt like saying, but she sat and let Mr. Mooney do the talking.

"You can go now," he said, opening the office door for her.

Tanya still sat in the secretary's chair. Melanie shot her a mean look as she passed by. She heard Mr. Mooney call Tanya into the office.

At hometime Miss Ryan stopped Melanie on her way out the door. "Are you okay, Melanie?" she asked.

Melanie nodded. Why couldn't they all just leave her alone?

"Is your mom going to be able to come in to see me?"

Melanie shrugged and sidled out the door.

Melanie's Birthday

*V*ictoria poured a second cup of coffee. "Monday morning already," she groaned.

Frances yawned in agreement.

Melanie didn't mind. She tugged her jacket on over a bulky knit sweater Victoria had given her and with a goodbye yell was out the apartment door to meet Rachel. Running around the side of the building, she noticed her breath hanging in puffs in the air.

Although several days had passed since Melanie and Rachel had discovered how close they lived to each other, Melanie was still thrilled every time she took the short-cut Rachel had shown her. Across the parking lot and down the back alley she sprinted, feeling the frosty air nip her ears.

The sky was grey this morning, the kind of grey that meant it could snow at any time. She wished it would, even though she didn't have winter clothes yet. She spotted Rachel in front of her apartment building, hopping up and down to keep warm while she waited.

Was that a new jacket Rachel was wearing? Forgetting to check for traffic Melanie bolted across the street, waving to her friend as she ran. She dashed up the slight incline to where Rachel waited for her and called out, "You got a new jacket! Is it ever nice!" She took Rachel by the arm. "Turn around and let me see the back!" she said, admiring the deep pink coat with turquoise trim around the pockets and cuffs. A similar pattern zigzagged across the back.

Rachel stuck her nose in the air and obliged Melanie by turning slowly and striking a model's pose. "You can try it on at recess," she promised.

Melanie rubbed the fur on the hood and smiled at the thought of snuggling into the furry pink lining. When would her mom be able to buy her a new winter jacket, she wondered.

But nothing could dampen her spirits today. "Guess what!" she said to Rachel, and without waiting for an answer, raced on. "This Thursday is my birthday! I'll be eleven."

"You lucky duck!" Rachel cried. "Mine's not till December."

"I probably won't be able to have a party though, Mom said – not until she finds us a place to live."

Rachel stopped in her tracks. "I got an idea. Why don't you sleep over with me?"

"On a school night? Are you kidding? My mom would never let me."

"Oh yeah, that's right, mine wouldn't either. But maybe we could on the weekend. I'll ask my mom and you ask yours, okay?"

Melanie bobbed her head in agreement.

The girls chattered about what they would do on their sleepover until they reached the schoolyard. The bell had rung so they hurried inside. "Don't tell anyone about my birthday," Melanie whispered to Rachel as they hung their coats. Rachel nodded okay.

Melanie took her seat. She wondered if her mom had any money to even buy her a present this year. She didn't mention this to Rachel, though. She probably shouldn't be thinking about presents at all when her mother needed money to find them a place to live. Still, she couldn't help hoping.

The class knew about her birthday anyway.

Miss Ryan had added her name to the birthday chart on the wall by the blackboard. It was a colourful poster of a big birthday cake with candles. Around the sides of the poster were the months of the year and under each month the names of students having birthdays. There was Melanie's name, under October. She'd noticed the birthday chart last week and had thought it was pretty, but now she wished her name wasn't on it.

However, as she usually did on Mondays, Miss Ryan checked the chart before starting class. She smiled at Melanie. "I see we have a birthday this week."

Melanie, sitting chin in hand, lowered her eyes and doodled on her desk with her pencil. A few minutes later she was rubbing her finger over the marks to erase them when a piece of paper dropped onto her desk. Melanie looked up to see Tanya walk past. She frowned. Not even a look had passed between them since their fight. Was Tanya trying to start something? As Melanie opened the note her eyes followed the girl back to her desk.

The scrap of paper was covered with little hearts Tanya had drawn and coloured, and at the bottom was a shiny sticker of a friendly laughing sun. It was pretty, even though it looked as if it had been peeled off something else and stuck there. Melanie read:

Can I play with you at recess

Your Friend
Tanya

Melanie blinked at the word "friend." This note couldn't be for her! She glanced across the room to see if Tanya realized where she'd dropped the paper. The note was no mistake; Tanya was looking right at her waiting for an answer, Melanie realized. Caught off guard, she nodded to Tanya, who flashed back a movie star smile and swung around in her desk.

Hastily Melanie turned the scrap of paper over and scribbled on the back to Rachel:

Tanya *wants to play with us at recess is that okay with you*

Melanie waited as Rachel scanned both sides of the paper. She turned around to Melanie then, arched her eyebrows until they disappeared under her bangs, and shrugged her shoulders up to her ears. "I don't care," she whispered, "but she'd better not try to start anything."

At recess Tanya waited for them at the coat rack. She twirled a piece of hair around her finger, and looked nervous. "Where do you want to play?" she asked.

Rachel zipped up her new jacket. "Let's go to the bridge," she said. Melanie was grateful Rachel hadn't offered to let her try on her new coat in front of Tanya.

The girls dashed outside and headed for the swinging bridge. As they stomped hard to make it sway back and forth Tanya asked Melanie, "What are you going to do for your birthday?"

Melanie replied, "I don't know." She wasn't lying; her mother hadn't said anything at all about her birthday. To escape from Tanya she staggered across the bridge toward Rachel, who was about to climb the tire tower.

However, Tanya stuck to her like a blob of gum. Right behind Melanie, she persisted, in an annoying wheedling tone, "If you invite me to your party I'll bring you a nice present."

"I'll see." Melanie's voice was terse. She wasn't going to tell Tanya she couldn't have a party.

During the next few days it seemed every kid in the class asked Melanie what she was doing for her birthday. She would turn her head away, and pretending to be doing something, she would say, "I don't know yet."

By Wednesday evening Melanie wished she didn't have a birthday at all. She wondered if she could be sick Thursday morning. She felt sick already, sick of all this fuss. Last year when she lived with *Kōhkom* her birthday wasn't such a big thing. Everyone teased her that she was getting too big to sleep with *Kōhkom*. And her mother said that she didn't have a baby any more. If there wasn't money for a present, she got one when there was, even if it was long after her real birthday.

Melanie worried till bedtime. She lay awake on the floor after the lights had been turned out and tried to think of the best way to get out of going to school in the morning. At last she decided she would have pains in her stomach.

Having stared at the ceiling for half the night she didn't wake until her mother shook her several times. "Wake up, birthday girl!"

Melanie groaned. Then as her mom bent to kiss her cheek, there was the rustle of a plastic bag near her pillow. She reached for it, but her mother pulled it away, saying, "I need a birthday kiss first."

Stomach pains forgotten, Melanie planted a

kiss on her cheek and grabbed at the bag. Everything fell out on the floor – eraser, pen, pencils, notebook, ruler, and best of all, pencil crayons, not even sharpened. Holding them in her hands she leaped at her mom, gripping her in a bear hug and knocking Frances off the edge of the sofa. The two fell in a heap on the floor and lay there laughing until Victoria came to see what was going on.

Melanie rose to her knees. "Look, Victoria! See what I got!"

"Snazzy stuff," Victoria said, as Melanie poked each item in her face before dropping it back into the bag. "Do you want to invite Rachel to supper this evening?"

Melanie looked at her mother. "Can I, Mom?" She held her breath until Frances nodded her head.

"Can we have hamburgers?"

"Hamburgers it is!" Victoria said, giving her untidy braid a gentle yank.

Eager to show Rachel her present and invite her to supper, Melanie allowed her mother to brush out her hair and braid it again so she could be finished faster.

Frances picked up a strand of hair. She said to Melanie, "I can't afford runners right now, my girl. Maybe at the end of the month."

Melanie didn't care. She danced out the door, proudly swinging her bag.

Rachel was as excited as Melanie about the supper invitation. And she wanted to see every single thing in Melanie's bag, which made them almost late for school. "We can use these in art today," Melanie said, poking her pencil crayons away.

Although class hadn't yet started they were the last to take their seats. Melanie laid her bag on top of the desk.

Tanya called across the room, "What did you get for your birthday?"

One by one Melanie pulled them out – red pen, notebook, eraser, blue pen, ruler, another notebook, glue, pencil crayons….

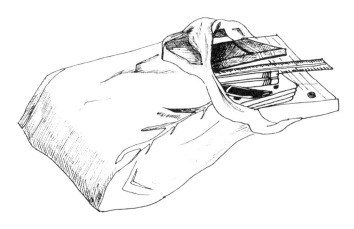

She'd only arranged half of it on her desk when Tanya's voice rang throughout the room. "That's all you got for your birthday? School supplies?"

Melanie froze, her hand in the bag.

The room went deathly still. The class held its breath, forever it seemed. Then Miss Ryan's voice slashed through the silence. "Tanya, come here."

Tanya clumped up to the teacher's desk, her shrill voice protesting, "I didn't *do* anything. I'm telling my mom."

Miss Ryan took her by the arm and removed her from the room.

But for Melanie it didn't matter. She was right back to that first day of school when those twenty pairs of eyes stared at her. Sitting stiff and straight, except for her bowed head, she crumpled the bag and shoved it inside her desk. Then in a dazed mechanical motion she swept everything into a heap and put them into her desk too.

While the girls, and some of the boys, muttered about what they'd like to do to Tanya, Melanie, without a word, took out her math book and opened it to where they'd left off yesterday. And when Rachel turned around,

Melanie avoided her eyes by searching in her desk for a pencil. When she found it she clutched it in both fists as if she might break it in half.

Ten minutes into math class she still hadn't made a single mark in her new notebook, though everyone else was busy with a seatwork assignment. Rachel kept turning around, her eyes as sad as an abandoned puppy's.

Melanie closed her notebook to hide her empty page and walked to the back table where the teacher was correcting work. "May I go to the washroom?" she asked, her voice and face expressionless.

Miss Ryan nodded.

Melanie turned her back on the teacher's concerned eyes.

Halfway down the hall, a voice behind her called, "Don't go into the janitor's room." Melanie looked back and Rachel ran to catch up to her. "Are you okay, Melanie?" she asked gently, laying her hand on Melanie's arm.

Melanie shrugged, but she didn't pull away. The girls were a sombre pair as they walked toward the washroom. Inside, neither spoke as they leaned against the wall. Melanie blinked back tears, more furious with herself for almost giving in to tears than she was with that witch,

Tanya. She didn't know if she wanted to beat Tanya up or run as far from this place as she could.

Then Rachel started to laugh. When Melanie looked at her she covered her mouth, but couldn't stifle it. Apologetically she explained, "My little brother, Adam, tried to flush his twin down the toilet this morning!"

"What?" A laugh caught in Melanie's throat. "How did that happen?"

"Well, my mom was putting on her make-up and she wasn't paying any attention to them…."

Melanie's eyes met Rachel's and the two girls doubled over laughing. Melanie held onto the basin to keep from falling. Still laughing, she wiped her eyes. "I'm gonna wet my pants," she cried helplessly.

"Oh, come on," Rachel giggled, "it's not that funny!" Then holding her stomach and laughing even harder, she said, "Maybe we should flush Tanya down the toilet!"

This brought on a new fit of giggles until finally, exhausted, the girls slid down to the floor to catch their breath. At last Rachel sighed: "Maybe it's time we went back."

Tanya had to do her work in the principal's office with no recess breaks, the kids said.

Melanie didn't care. The rest of the day was a blur, a long dreary one. Her head ached the whole afternoon. She used her new stuff. But Tanya had ruined the fun. If she could have one birthday wish, it would be that she could be back in Elk Crossing. She'd walk home from school with Keena, right into *Kōhkom*'s kitchen.

Even the thought of Rachel coming to supper couldn't lighten Melanie's heart or lessen the pain that gripped the top of her head.

"See you in an hour," she called, as she left Rachel by her building after school. Melanie shuffled along, examining every tree overhanging the alley, aiming a stone at every garbage can. But in spite of her dawdling she reached the end of the alley and Victoria's apartment was only a parking lot away. She rang the buzzer and waited, not caring if she ever got inside.

Her mother answered so quickly she must have been standing by the intercom. "My girl, is that you?" Frances always yelled through the speaker, even though Melanie had told her over and over to just talk in her normal voice.

"Let me in." The buzz that allowed Melanie to enter still sounded as she turned the knob of the apartment door. Though she'd shown her mom at least a half dozen times how long to hold down the button, Frances couldn't seem to get the hang of it.

"*Kinipa*, Melanie," Frances peered out into the hallway.

"What do you want?" Melanie asked, following her mother into the apartment.

Frances took the bag out of her hand and waltzed with it through the short hallway to the living room.

Melanie followed. She laughed, in spite of herself. Her mother looked so funny. Then Frances turned, caught Melanie in her arms and danced her in a circle through the living room, kitchen, hallway, and back to the living room again. Melanie was laughing too much to ask what was going on, but she had a feeling this wasn't all due to her birthday.

Breathless, Frances fell on the sofa pulling Melanie down with her. While she patted her bosom and gasped for air, Melanie begged, "Tell me, what is it?"

Frances struggled to sit up. She smoothed her hair and tugged her blouse down over her hips. "I found a house for us today!"

Too shocked for words, Melanie stared at her mother as if she'd just grown another head.

Frances took Melanie's chin in her hand and

looked into her face. "You don't look very happy. I thought you'd be excited."

Melanie faked a smile. "I'm just surprised," she said.

"Do you want to go see it?" her mother asked.

"You mean right now?"

Frances stood up and pulled her off the couch. "Right now."

"I have to go to the bathroom first."

"Well, hurry then."

Melanie closed the bathroom door. She didn't need to go to the bathroom. She needed to think, but her thoughts were so confused. She didn't want to move again. She liked living with Victoria. And if her mother moved into her own place Melanie was stuck here in the city for sure. And she'd promised *Kōhkom* she'd be back. Her head was pounding. Everything was getting worse.

Her mother called to her then and she opened the door.

Searching for a way to get out of having to see the place, she said, "But what about Rachel? She's coming to supper."

"It won't take long. The house is just a few blocks away. Call Rachel and tell her you'll phone her when you get back."

Melanie, unable to come up with another excuse, went to the phone.

Rachel answered. On hearing the news she had a million questions for Melanie. But Melanie cut her off. "I'll call you when we get back and you can come right over," she said, her voice sounding flat to her own ears.

On the way down the street Frances talked about the house and how she would start looking in second-hand stores for some furniture.

Frances left the sidewalk and walked across a narrow gravel driveway scraped out of the east side of a small square of lawn. "It's this one," she said. A runt of a house, peak-roofed like a box with the lids left up, squatted on the remaining bit of land.

"It's nice," Melanie said. It was, too, she admitted grudgingly to herself. Just like a doll's house. "Can we go inside?" she asked.

"No, I don't have keys yet. Here, I'll stand on the step and hoist you up so you can look through the window."

Melanie, gripped around the hips, leaned to the side and cupped her hands around her eyes. She peered into a small room that held a fridge and stove. "This is the kitchen," she announced, and slid down to her feet. "Can I look in that window?" She pointed along the front of the house.

"No, my girl, it's too high. And you're too heavy," her mother teased.

"I wonder how far it is from Rachel's place?" Melanie asked on the way back to Victoria's.

"It's a bit farther," her mother told her.

She ran ahead of her mom back into the apartment and dialed Rachel's number. "I'll meet you in the alley right away," she said.

When Rachel asked what the house was like, Melanie said, "I'll tell you when I see you," and slammed down the receiver.

A few minutes later they met in the alley. "Now tell me about the house," Rachel said. "Is it near here?"

"It's a bit farther, but we can still walk it."

"What's it like?"

"Well, my mom doesn't have keys yet, so we couldn't go inside. But it's small and white. It reminds me of a doll's house."

Rachel's piercing black eyes bored into her face. "You don't sound very excited. I thought that was what you wanted."

Melanie sighed and jammed her hands into her jacket pocket. "That's what my mom wanted, but…."

"But what?"

"Well, I like living with Victoria. She's nice. And if we move into a house I'm afraid we'll never go back home."

"But your mom is only staying here while she goes to school, isn't she? Then you'll go back."

"But that's a long time. I don't want to be away from home that long." She looked at Rachel's perplexed face. "Besides, I'll be farther away from you, too."

"Silly, you're only moving a few blocks. You'll still see Victoria lots. And we'll look for another short-cut."

She linked her arm through Melanie's. "When are you moving in?"

"Tomorrow night."

"Oh, that means you won't be able to sleep over." Rachel sounded disappointed.

Melanie had completely forgotten about their plan. To make up to Rachel she said, "Maybe you could sleep over at my place next weekend. I'll ask my mom." Rachel seemed happy with that.

By the time they reached the apartment door Melanie felt better. The girls helped make the hamburger patties while Frances popped frozen fries into the oven. Victoria arrived home from work with soft drinks and soon they were eating supper. Towards the end of the meal Frances disappeared and came back holding a rectangular cake pan, which she set in the centre of the table.

Melanie's eyes widened. She looked at the cake, iced and decorated with eleven candles, all colours. She grinned and leaned over for a closer look. "Where did you hide it? I didn't see it in the fridge."

"That's my secret." Frances winked at Rachel.

Rachel sat back in her chair. "I'm stuffed," she said. "I think I'm too full for cake …"

Victoria agreed. "I'm full too." She looked at Melanie. "How about if we open the presents first and have cake after?"

"More presents?" Melanie didn't need to think twice. She pushed back her chair and pranced to the living room after Victoria.

Rachel went to her jacket pocket and returned with a tiny package which she handed to Melanie. "Happy Birthday, Melanie!"

"Thanks, Rachel!" Melanie ripped it open. "My own nail polish! What a pretty colour!"

"My mom bought it at the drugstore today," Rachel said.

With a flourish Victoria set another package in front of her. Melanie beamed and tore it open.

She and Rachel oohed over the red hair band and several fancy hair elastics, trimmed with beads and bows. "Thank you, thank you, thank you," she told Victoria, exclaiming over each one.

Frances gathered up the paper. "And you don't have to help with the dishes after," she added, planting a kiss on Melanie's flushed cheek.

Melanie, sitting on the carpet, smiled up at her. "Thanks, Mom."

While Victoria and Frances washed the dishes she and Rachel spread an old newspaper on the coffee table and set about doing each other's nails. They had just finished and were blowing on their fingernails to dry them faster when Frances called, "Come and have some cake."

Victoria rooted around in her purse until she found a pack of matches. She lit all the candles but two before blowing out the match. Passing the pack to Melanie she said, "Here, you and Rachel can light the last two."

Gingerly the girls each lit a candle.

"We'll count to three," Victoria said to Melanie. "Close your eyes and make a wish."

Melanie looked around the table. If Keena

and *Kōhkom* were here the evening would be just about perfect. She closed her eyes.

Everyone counted. "One."

She couldn't make a wish; she'd already made it in school this afternoon. For some weird reason Tanya's mean face flashed across her mind.

"Two."

Then she saw *Kōhkom*, looking so lonely. She drew in a shaky breath.

"Three."

She started to blow. But instead a monster sob came out. And close behind, too close to stop them, were the tears. A pailful at least.

Nobody could make her feel better, no matter what they said. Her birthday was ruined. This time there was no one to blame. She had done it all by herself.

The House

*T*he next day after school Melanie walked into the apartment to find her mother folding clothes, still hot from the dryer. As Frances packed their bag, she said, "Well, my girl, I hope this is the last move for a while."

Melanie sighed, so loud it was more like a groan. "Me too," she said. Unless it's back home, she added to herself.

Shortly after, Victoria arrived home lugging several boxes she'd picked up at the corner store. She made herself a cup of coffee and let it sit on the counter while she hunted through the cupboards and stacked an assortment of dishes on the table. Melanie was set to work packing them into a box. "Stuff some newspaper in there too," Victoria said, pointing to a pile on the floor by the chesterfield. She drained her coffee and absent-mindedly set it on the table with the mugs to be packed.

Melanie moved it aside so she wouldn't forget and pack it with the others. She stuffed a wad of paper down the side of the box.

"You know, I'm really going to miss you two," Victoria said. "This place will be as empty as the band office at three o'clock on payday."

Frances laughed. "Ah, you'll be thankful for some peace and quiet," she said. "Besides, we'll be here so often you'll think you only dreamed we moved out. Right, my girl?"

Melanie nodded. It was nice to hear Victoria say she would miss them too. She closed the lid of the box as Victoria and Frances piled quilts on the table.

"You can use these for as long as you need them," Victoria said, pouring more coffee for herself and Frances. "Now let's have some supper before we go over to the house." She opened the fridge door. "I guess it'll have to be my Friday night special." She lifted a corner of plastic wrap from the bowl she held and sniffed. "Stew still smells okay." Then she pulled out a small plastic container and removing the lid, tipped it so that Melanie could see the meat patty inside.

"Want a moose burger?" she asked.

"Sure," Melanie replied.

By the time they'd eaten and cleaned up it was dark already. They drove in a taxi to the house and, with the three of them each carrying an armful, they moved in.

The entrance, as tiny as a phone booth, allowed only enough room for Melanie and her mom to squeeze in to unlock the front door which opened into the living room. Victoria had to stay on the steps until they were in.

The room they entered wasn't all that much bigger.

And the all-white walls and almost white patternless linoleum, cold under Melanie's sock feet, didn't make it seem any larger, just emptier. There wasn't a stick of furniture, not one curtain. A crooked crack ran across the ceiling plaster and a gaping window looked out onto the street.

Somehow Melanie couldn't quite picture the bony old tree over in the corner of the yard in spring bloom. All she could see were its gnarled limbs. The world outside looked just as bare as the rooms inside. A feeling of loneliness filled her, driving her from the window.

She wandered through the house. Next to the living room was the kitchen. Unlike the bare living room it held an old fridge and stove. It too was small. There would hardly be enough room to squeeze in a table, if they got one.

Next to the living room on the other side was a bedroom and another one at the top of the narrow flight of stairs. Melanie decided she didn't want to sleep up there alone. She and her mother could share the downstairs bedroom.

"When are we going to get some furniture?" she asked.

"As soon as I have some money," her mom replied. She shoved a box of blankets into the bedroom with her foot. "It'll be a while though. We'll have to camp. And I know you like to camp."

Her voice was bright, but it rang fake. Melanie wasn't fooled. She knew her mother was just trying to act excited for her sake. She felt like saying, "And I know you don't." But she held her tongue, only because Victoria was there. Her mother hated camping. She never came with them when they went to *Mosōm*'s old fishing camp at Minstik Lake. Uncle Pierre used it since *Mosōm* died and every summer Melanie, *Kōhkom*, and Uncle's family spent a couple of weeks there. But not her mother. She'd heard *Kōhkom* grumble once to Uncle that it was too quiet there for her mom. Well, it would sure be quiet here. They didn't even have a radio or a TV. She'd watch and see how her mother liked camping.

After Victoria left, Frances unpacked the quilts and spread them out on the bedroom floor. She covered the window with a sheet.

Melanie put the few dishes in the cupboard and the cutlery in the drawer. Their single pot she placed on the stove.

Then they walked down the street to the store and bought some bread, milk, teabags, and other food for the morning. Melanie's mother told her to choose a chocolate bar from a bin where they were marked on sale.

Melanie ripped off the wrapper the minute they were outside. Her mother refused her offer of a bite. Melanie munched on the chocolate, deciding to be nice all evening. She looked up the street at the house, all lit up, and stopped suddenly, right in front of her mom, almost tripping her.

"What are you doing?" her mother asked, steadying herself.

"I'm looking at the house," Melanie said. "It looks kind of cosy with the lights on."

Frances smiled at her and nodded. "Yes, it does, " she agreed. "But if you're going to stop like that again, give me some warning, please."

Melanie chuckled as she ran to the door.

Frances made a kitchen table by turning a box upside down and placing a towel over it. It worked well, Melanie thought.

They had a snack before going to bed. Her mother made toast by putting a slice of bread on a wire hanger she found and holding it over the burner until it browned. They boiled water for tea in the pot and added a teabag. Melanie sipped her mug of hot tea slowly; her mom was doing okay at camping so far, she admitted grudgingly to herself.

At bedtime her mother said, "Tomorrow we'll call *Kōhkom* and tell her we found a place."

"But how? *Kōhkom* doesn't have a phone."

"I'll phone Pauline's and someone will go get her. Then I'll call back and we'll talk to her."

How could she be expected to go to sleep after that?

Melanie fidgeted under her blankets until her mother said, "Melanie, lie still and go to sleep."

Sleep, however, was the farthest thing from Melanie's mind. Images of *Kōhkom* loomed in her head. She hoped whoever went to get her grandmother would help her up the hill to Pauline's house. It was steep for *Kōhkom* with her bad legs, and the path had lots of loose gravel. Finally, Melanie worried herself into a fitful sleep, waking several times during the night, stiff, uncovered, and cold.

Then, just after dawn, she drifted off into a dream she didn't want to leave. There was just her and *Kōhkom*; it was like they were floating somewhere. All she could see was *Kōhkom*'s loving face smiling fully at her. She felt *Kōhkom* caress her head and clip a barrette in her hair. She knew the barrette was very, very beautiful, but woke up before she could see it. Eyes closed, she lay there, trying to stay in the dream but, no matter how she tried, it was gone. Then she noticed her eyelids were wet.

When her mom called she stirred as if she were just waking. She didn't tell her mother about the dream, but all morning it stayed in her mind. *Kōhkom* sometimes talked about dreams. Before *Mosōm* died *Kōhkom* had dreamed she was giving him herb tea to make him feel better, but he had looked at her and pushed the mug away. Melanie hoped her grandmother was okay.

She couldn't wait to phone. Finally, the afternoon came and they walked over to Victoria's apartment. Melanie nagged until she was permitted to dial her cousin's phone number.

Frances called each digit out to her, in spite of Melanie's protests that she had the paper with the number on it right in front of her. Mom reminded Melanie of a bingo caller.

Melanie was relieved when she heard her mother talking to *Kōhkom*. Everything seemed to be all right. She waited forever for the end of the conversation. She tugged on her mom's arm, but Frances nodded and went right on talking. Finally, Melanie had the phone in her hands.

"*Tānisi, Kōhkom*," she said."*Melanie awa.*"

Her grandmother spoke pure Cree. After saying her name over and over she asked, "How is school?"

"Fine," Melanie replied. She didn't mention Rachel. *Kōhkom* couldn't hear well over the phone and a lot of conversation confused her.

"Do you like the new house?" *Kōhkom* asked.

"Fine."

"Be a good girl now. Help your mom."

"Okay *Kōhkom*. I love you." Melanie passed the phone back.

She sank into Victoria's couch and bit at a piece of skin by her thumbnail while her mother finished her conversation. Talking to *Kōhkom* hadn't been a bit like the television commercials, which said long distance was the next best thing to being there. Her grandmother's wise, old eyes could take one look at Melanie and know exactly what she was feeling. But not over the phone. She thought she knew now why *Kōhkom* had never liked phones.

Victoria set the crib board on the table, and she and Frances settled down to play a few games of cards. Melanie wandered from the table to the television and then to the phone. She called Rachel every five minutes or so but there was no answer. Slumped in front of the television, she resigned herself to not seeing Rachel until Monday.

On Monday morning she wore a house key around her neck. She and her mother left the house together. Frances had an appointment at the training centre. Melanie knew she was nervous about it. She changed her top twice and didn't even sit down to drink her coffee.

Frances waited at the bus stop at the end of the block, while Melanie turned the corner to walk to school. Her mother called after her, "Come straight home after school ... and make sure you lock the door."

Melanie ran most of the way, eager to see Rachel. Spotting her crossing the street to the playground Melanie yelled her friend's name until Rachel turned around. "Wait up!" Melanie shouted still half a block away.

Rachel walked back to meet her. "My mom said I could go to your place after school."

"Oh, good," Melanie replied.

"But I have to leave at four-thirty, so I'll be home before dark."

"We'll still have an hour," Melanie said.

At 3:35 they trotted briskly up Eleventh Avenue so that they'd have as much of the hour as possible. Melanie showed Rachel around the house. Then she buttered some bannock for them and they ate at the makeshift box table. "It's just like camping," Rachel grinned.

Four-thirty came too soon. Rachel left just a few minutes late, promising, "I'll ask my mom if you can come to my place after school tomorrow and she can drop you off when she gets home."

"Okay," Melanie said, "I'll ask my mom too."

With Rachel gone she watched the window for her mother. The house creaked and sighed in ways she'd never heard before. Kneeling by the window, Melanie looked over her shoulder, not daring to find out what the noises were. Though it was actually only an hour, it seemed like much longer before she spotted her mother at the end of the block.

Melanie flung open the door and stood

shivering and hugging her arms until her mother entered the house. Like a stray pup, she followed her mom from closet to kitchen as Frances hung up her coat and got a drink of water from the kitchen tap. Frances laid her glass in the sink. "I'll be late tomorrow, Melanie."

"Later than this? How come?"

Frances turned from the sink and catching Melanie's cheeks between her hands, rubbed her nose on Melanie's. "Because, my girl, I have some tests to write. Your mother has been accepted for school."

Melanie heard the elation in her mother's voice. She struggled to free herself. All she felt was despair.

Fighting tears, she walked over to the window and stared out into the darkness. They had a house. And now her mother was starting school. She might as well give up. She was never getting out of the city.

No Money

"But that's good news, Melanie! I don't see why you're so upset."

"Good news. Are you crazy, Rachel? Now I'll never get back to Elk Crossing."

"Use your little brain, Melanie. Now that your mom's in school, you'll get back faster."

"Yeah, right."

"Sure, you will. My mom had to wait almost a year before she even got into school."

Melanie looked at her friend. "Did she really?"

"Yes, she did." Rachel nodded her head vigorously.

Melanie grinned at her friend. Sometimes Rachel reminded her of Keena. When *Kōhkom* had gotten sick with high blood pressure it had been Keena who had made her see the bright side. She'd told Melanie she should be thankful that *Kōhkom* wasn't worse, that she didn't have to go to the hospital.

And here was Rachel doing the same thing. Maybe it *was* good that her mother got into school right away.

She and Rachel spent most of their free time together now. One afternoon after school they were digging around in the scrap-box at the back of the class for some good paper. Rachel caught Melanie's eye and nodded towards the shelf above their heads where there were three apples, a couple of muffins, and half a sandwich wrapped in cellophane. Baffled, Melanie whispered a hoarse, "What?"

Rachel bent towards her. "Let's take the muffins to your place for a snack."

Melanie shook her head and darted a look toward the desk where Miss Ryan worked. The teacher's head was bent over a book. "No," she whispered, barely moving her lips. "I'm leaving."

So Rachel had noticed there was hardly any food at her house, not enough for after school snacks. Feeling her face grow hot and knowing she was turning as red as a raspberry, Melanie escaped from Rachel and the classroom.

She was already out the door when Rachel

caught up with her. "What's the matter with you? The teacher said it's okay."

Melanie gasped. She stopped still and looked at Rachel. "You asked her?"

"Well, the way you acted you made it seem like I wanted to steal. Melanie, the teacher said last week when we started collecting lunchtime leftovers that she hated to see good food go in the garbage. That food is for anybody, and I don't see anything wrong with eating it." She reached into the plastic bag that held their paper, found an apple, and took a huge bite out of it. "Mm-mm-mm, good!" she said. "Want one?"

Rachel looked so determined Melanie burst out laughing. Then she too reached into the bag and found an apple. "What did the teacher say?"

"I said, 'Miss Ryan, is it okay if I take the leftovers for a snack for me and Melanie?' And she said, 'Go right ahead. It'll have to go in the garbage if someone doesn't eat it.'" Rachel took another bite. Then she said, "So I took it all. We can have the muffins when we get to your house."

Melanie munched on her apple, trying to find the right words to tell Rachel that there wasn't much money for food or anything until her mom got paid for going to school.

Rachel interrupted her thoughts. "I remember when we first moved here before my mom started school, my Uncle Sol had to buy us some food. And he told us about the Food Bank."

"Food Bank. What's that?" Melanie was curious.

"It's a place downtown, where you can get free food if you don't have any money to buy some. We went there until my mom started getting some money."

"I wonder if Mom would go? Is it still there?"

"Sure. I'll get the address for you."

The next evening as Frances added salt to the flour soup, a broth with a taste of meat and some macaroni in it, Melanie pulled the address of the Food Bank out of her pocket. "Rachel gave me this." She shoved the paper in her mother's face practically. "It's called the Food Bank and you can get food there for nothing if you have no money."

Frances glanced at the paper. She stopped stirring.

Melanie waited for her to say something. It shouldn't take this long to read a few words; her mother wasn't that far behind in school. But Frances wasn't reading. Melanie could tell that her mom's eyes weren't even seeing the words.

Then she realized Frances didn't like the idea of going to the Food Bank. The tightening around her mother's mouth told her. Without a word, Melanie left her standing at the stove. She was only trying to help.

However, the next evening Frances arrived home with two bags of groceries. "That has to last until the end of the month," was all she said.

Melanie hummed a tune she'd learned in music class as she put the food in the cupboard.

She was no longer shy to take leftovers from the shelf at school and often saved a muffin to share with her mom for dessert. With Victoria dropping by every now and then with some moose meat or bannock, they managed to stretch the food for quite a while. But close to the end of the month, there was nothing to take to school for lunch.

Frances checked the fridge, though she knew there was nothing inside. "I guess I'll have to ask

Victoria to lend me twenty dollars until the funding at school comes through," she muttered as she felt around the bottom of her purse for coins for the bus.

Melanie knew she hated to ask Victoria for money. "It's okay, Mom," she said, "Lots of kids eat lunch at the hall."

"You sure?" Frances didn't look convinced.

"Yes, I'm sure." Melanie put on her most sincere face and looked straight at her mom.

At noon, she lingered around the school, waiting for the way to be clear before crossing the street to the hall. She gazed north toward the river and thought how it must be all frozen by now. A rush of loneliness, like a strong undertow, tugged at her insides, unsettling her. She made a face, as if she had a bitter taste in her mouth, stuck out her chin and pulled open the door of the church hall.

Each time she went there Melanie felt that awful feeling in the pit of her stomach as she pulled open the door. She always sat alone, uncomfortable in this place. In spite of everyone's attempts to be friendly, she ate as fast as she could and escaped before the other kids could finish their lunches and come outside for the noon break. She didn't even tell Rachel where she went for lunch and Rachel, though she must have known, didn't ask.

A few days later the teacher asked Melanie to wait after school so she could talk to her. Rachel waited outside.

In the quiet emptiness of the classroom Miss Ryan seemed to be searching for words. "Melanie, is everything okay?"

Melanie had no idea what the teacher was talking about. "Yes," she said.

"Do you have food at home?"

"Yes," Melanie lied.

The teacher fumbled on. "Well, I noticed you've been leaving at lunchtime and I talked to Mrs. McKay and she said you've been going to the hall for lunch regularly."

Melanie shrugged and looked at the floor.

"And I noticed you've been taking the leftovers …"

Melanie lifted her head and stared at the wall. "If you don't want me to have them, I won't take any more." She hardly recognized the dull voice as her own.

"Oh no, that's not what I mean." The teacher sounded flustered. "You're certainly welcome to them. I was just wondering if there's anything I can do to help?"

Feeling trapped, Melanie shook her head. Her eyes turned toward the door, desperate to get out of there.

Miss Ryan, looking every bit as uncomfortable as Melanie, let her go.

The next morning Melanie woke with a sore throat.

She could hardly swallow. Her head hurt so bad, even blinking was painful. And for the first time, there was no *Kōhkom* to make her feel better.

She didn't tell her mom. She didn't want to stay home alone, and she didn't want Frances to miss school. And in the rush of the morning her mother didn't notice.

At recess she snuck into the washroom and sat in a cubicle shivering until the bell rang. By now her neck and back were aching too. She felt so miserable she could barely keep from crying. Still, she refused to let Rachel tell the teacher.

At snacktime she felt too awful even to eat her cheese and crackers.

Miss Ryan saw the misery in her eyes and asked, "Are you feeling okay, Melanie?"

Rachel said, "She's sick. She has a sore throat and headache."

Melanie wished Rachel hadn't said anything, but it was too late now.

Miss Ryan wanted to send her home right away but Melanie told the teacher that her mom was at school and wouldn't be home till five. She looked up at the teacher. "I'm okay, honest," she lied.

That evening Melanie didn't have to say anything. She was lying on the blankets when her mother walked in.

One look at Melanie told Frances that something was wrong. "Melanie, why didn't you say something this morning?" she asked when she'd looked at Melanie's throat. "You need to see a doctor. We'll go to Victoria's and phone."

Melanie allowed her mother to bundle her up for the walk to Victoria's place. She felt absolutely wretched already and the walk just made her feel worse. Victoria phoned her doctor and was able to get Melanie in right away. She came with them to show the way and the bus took them right to the downtown clinic.

The doctor said she had strep throat and should stay home from school for three or four days. She also had to take a huge yellow and black capsule four times a day. Melanie saw Victoria lend her mom a twenty dollar bill to pay for the pills. Her mother looked so uncomfortable Melanie felt sorry for her.

That night Frances pondered what to do.

"I can stay home alone," Melanie reassured her through lips that could hardly move.

"No, my girl, I can't leave you here by yourself all day. But if I stay home I'll lose my pay, and we really need the money."

"I'll be okay. Besides, there's nothing else to do. Victoria works and we don't know anybody else."

"Wait a minute. I'll ask Lorraine. She'll let you stay at her place."

"No," Melanie whined. "I don't want to stay there."

There was no reply from her mother.

Melanie started to cry.

Frances laid down on the blankets by her. "Sh-sh, *nitānis*, crying will make you feel worse."

With an angry tug at the blankets Melanie turned away. "I don't care," she sobbed. "I don't want to go there."

Kōhkom would never do this to her. She'd never make Melanie stay somewhere she didn't like, especially when she was sick.

And if her mother made her go there she'd be sorry.

Visitors

*M*elanie leaned against the shabby arm of Lorraine's worn-out chesterfield, and tucked her feet under her. She couldn't get comfortable. Whenever she moved, the brown cushions, stained and shapeless, slid away from her and her feet dug into the broken springs poking through underneath.

She stood up and stuffed them back into place. Even then the cushions lay lopsided, like air mattresses tossing in the wake of speedboat waves. Crawling back onto the couch as carefully as if she were climbing into a canoe, she caught sight of someone out front. She looked closer and saw two women, one following the other up the narrow walk to the house. They stopped and looked at a piece of paper as if they weren't sure of the address. Who would be coming to visit Lorraine, Melanie wondered.

She didn't answer the first feeble knock. But the second rap was more insistent. Lorraine was upstairs; she'd been yelling at the boys a few minutes ago. Melanie twisted the loose door-knob back and forth until finally it caught and the door swung inward, grating on a patch of floor scraped bare of linoleum.

"Hello," said the shorter and wider of the two women, greeting Melanie as if she were a long-time friend she was glad to see again. "We're from McKenzie School. I'm Mrs. Fiddler." She was a grandmotherly figure, with a smile to match. "And this is Mrs. Henderson."

The tall woman with owl-eyed glasses and a perm woven as tight as a bird's nest smiled too. She bent over, as if apologizing for her height, and asked, "Are you Melanie?"

The cold air from the open door plucked on the hairs of Melanie's arms. She nodded, without returning their smiles. What did they want with her?

The tall woman said, "Your teacher was worried when you didn't come to school. She asked us to drop in and see you." She leaned closer; her eyes, magnified behind her thick glasses, were large with concern.

Mrs. Fiddler looked past Melanie into the room. "Is your mom home?"

Melanie shook her head, her hand still on the doorknob.

"Are you by yourself?"

"No," Melanie replied, "I'll get Lorraine."

Melanie retreated from the room. She heard the women step inside and close the door.

When she returned with Lorraine, the women shook the limp hand offered them and introduced themselves again before accepting Lorraine's hesitant invitation to sit down.

Mrs. Fiddler took her time and settled herself on the chesterfield, chatting all the while. "We're community workers from McKenzie," she told Lorraine. "We've come to see if everything is okay with Melanie." She went on in her kindly voice. "Miss Ryan was concerned when she didn't come to school and there was no phone call or anything to say where she was."

"We don't have a phone," Melanie said.

Mrs. Henderson pulled a notebook out of her bulky black purse and jotted something down. Melanie wondered if she was writing that they didn't have a phone.

Mrs. Fiddler said, "Your teacher told us your

throat was really sore the last day you were in school. Did you go see a doctor?"

Melanie nodded. Lorraine answered for her. "The doctor told her mom to keep her home for three or four days. She has pills to take."

"Oh, that's good. You'll feel better in no time." Mrs. Fiddler clucked like a mother hen.

"She's been staying here during the day, but she's feeling a lot better now. She should be back in school tomorrow."

Mrs. Henderson raised her eyebrows so that they sat on top of her heavy black frames like a brown trim. "You mean Melanie doesn't live here?"

"No," replied Melanie. Still standing, she crossed her arms and rocked back and forth on her ankles.

Mrs. Henderson bent her head and wrote some more. "How long ago did you move? This is the address we have on file." Her hand jerked across the sheet in an agitated manner.

Lorraine pursed her lips and shrugged. She sure wasn't acting too friendly. She got up from the arm of the chair and looked at her watch, like she wanted to get rid of the women as soon as she could.

But Melanie liked them. Grandmotherly

Mrs. Fiddler looked at her as if she'd like to take Melanie on her lap and cuddle her. Melanie gave them her sweetest smile. She replied, "I forgot to tell Mr. Mooney our new address when we moved."

Pen poised, Mrs. Henderson asked, "What is it, my dear?"

Melanie put her finger on her chin and cast her eyes toward the ceiling. "Do you mean this time, or the time before?"

Mrs. Henderson's eyebrows jumped up on her glasses again and Mrs. Fiddler patted the couch next to her. "Well, how many times have you moved, Melanie dear?"

Melanie, careful not to look at Lorraine, squeezed in between the two women. She had their undivided attention. She paused before answering. "Well, first we lived with my *Kōhkom*, and my mom made me come here with her. Then we lived here with Lorraine for a little while, and then we lived with Victoria for another little while, and then we moved to the empty house."

There was a thud from upstairs followed by shrieks. Lorraine ran from the room.

But the women had eyes only for her. "You mean there is no one living in the house but you and your mother?" asked Mrs. Henderson. Her eyebrows still had not come down.

Melanie was thoroughly enjoying herself. "Well, that too." She paused dramatically. "But I mean the house is empty. Really empty. No beds, no chairs, no table – no nothing." She looked at the ladies to see what they thought of that.

Mrs. Fiddler patted Melanie's hand. "Where is this house, Melanie?"

"The address is 643 Ninth Street West."

Mrs. Henderson scribbled energetically. Without looking up, she said, "Is your mom working?"

Melanie shook her head. "No, she's going to school. That's why I had to come and stay at Lorraine's house. There was no one home."

"Oh, I see. Do you know where your mom goes to school?"

Melanie shrugged and shook her head. The women looked at each other. Mrs. Henderson was speed-writing now. Melanie was amazed. The pen seemed to have a life of its own.

While she wrote Mrs. Fiddler explained, "It's important to have as much information as possible about all our families in case of emergencies." It sounded to Melanie that she was apologizing for Mrs. Henderson's eager questioning.

Finally, Mrs. Henderson closed her notebook. "Well then," she said, "that's about it." She gave Melanie a thoughtful look. "And what about you, Melanie? How do you feel about moving to the city?"

Melanie looked directly at the two women. Finally, someone was asking how she felt. "I miss my *Kōhkom*," she said. "I even had a dream about her. If I could I would go back home to Elk Crossing tomorrow."

Mrs. Henderson leaned toward Melanie. "And leave your mother behind?"

Melanie felt guilty for a half a second. But it was her mother who forced her to stay at Lorraine's stinky house this week. "Yes," she whispered, holding her throat as if it were still sore.

Mrs. Fiddler patted her hand again. "Are you sure you're feeling well enough to come to school tomorrow?"

Melanie nodded and stood up as the women got out of their chairs.

With her hand on the doorknob, Mrs. Fiddler spoke to Lorraine who, with a fresh cigarette in hand, had just reappeared. "Tell Mrs. Bluelake someone from the Native Family Counselling Centre will be dropping round – to see if she needs any help."

Lorraine nodded and closed the door behind them. "I hope you didn't say anything to get your mom in trouble, Melanie."

"Like what?" Melanie asked, feeling a little anxious now. She had talked a lot. But she tossed her head. It served her mother right.

"What's a counselling centre?" she asked Lorraine.

"It's a place that helps Indian people when they move into the city."

That sounded okay. If they were supposed to help Indian people for sure they wouldn't do anything bad. Would they?

Trouble

*F*rances reached into the cupboard for a bag of potatoes. "I have homework tonight," she said.

"What kind?" Melanie asked, grinning. She thought the idea of her mom doing homework funny.

"Math," her mom replied, passing her a knife to help peel. "I hope I still have a brain. It's been a long time since I did math."

Melanie couldn't help giggling at the idea of her mother without a brain. But when she looked she saw her mother wasn't laughing. Her face wore an anxious look as she sliced a potato in half.

She felt a sudden rush of affection for her mom, something she hadn't felt for a while. She laid her head against her mom's arm. "Don't worry, Mom. I'm good at math. I'll help you."

"*Ki nanāskomitin, nitānis*. I'm sure I'll need all the help I can get." Frances put the pot on the burner. "We'd better hurry. Did Lorraine say what time that lady from the counselling centre would be stopping by?"

"I don't think so," Melanie replied. Mention of the centre made her feel edgy.

"I wonder what she wants," Frances mused.

Melanie shrugged. "Can I see your math book?"

Her mother chinned. "Over there in the corner."

Later that evening when a knock sounded at their back door, Melanie said to her mother, "That must be the lady from the centre now." She followed Frances to the door.

Melanie was surprised to find that the woman standing on the step knew her mother. "*Tānisi*, Frances," she said. "It's been a long time since I saw you."

Frances returned the woman's greeting and called her Doris. She stood back to let her in. She told Melanie, "When Doris was growing up, she used to visit her granny in Elk Crossing."

Doris unbuttoned her jacket. "That was long before you were born," she said. She looked at Frances. "I moved to the city after high school and I've been a family worker at the centre ever since."

Melanie felt her mother relax as she talked to Doris and she began to be at ease too.

When Frances asked Doris if she'd like some tea, Melanie said, "I'll get it." As she put the water on to boil she listened to the conversation.

Frances chatted comfortably to Doris. "I can't depend on my mom to support us forever. It's time I started to look after myself, and Melanie. I'm doing upgrading right now to finish high school first," she said.

Doris listened mostly, nodding every now and then.

Then, as Melanie returned to the living room, she asked, "Are you having any money problems?"

Frances grimaced before she replied. "Money's tight. My school allowance hasn't come through yet." She took the mugs from Melanie and set them down on their improvised table. She apologized to Doris, "Sorry we can't offer you a chair. I thought I'd be able to find a place already furnished, but I couldn't. So I'll have to buy some second-hand furniture."

Doris nodded in sympathy. "Moving is hard," she said. Her eyes wandered to Melanie's summer jacket and old runners lying in the corner of the room.

"I have to get Melanie a winter jacket and some boots too," Frances said.

Doris was quiet. She sipped her tea without saying a word for a few minutes. Then, with her head tilted to one side, she looked at Frances for what seemed to Melanie like a long time before she said, "Maybe we can help you out."

"How? What can you do?" Frances asked.

Melanie was all ears. Doris looked at her but said nothing. It was then her mother sent her into the bedroom and told her to close the door. Melanie didn't want to go; she made a face at her mother as she left the room, and listened at the door.

"Why don't you let us take Melanie until you get on your feet?" Doris asked, keeping her voice low.

"She's not going anywhere." Frances' voice was shaking.

Melanie covered her mouth with her hand, unable to believe what she was hearing. What had she done? Lorraine was right. She should never have talked to those women. Her heart pounded in her chest louder, it seemed, than the words she strained to hear.

Doris went on. "No, I don't mean that we take custody of her. She can stay at the residence until you can take care of her."

Melanie had heard about the student residence. It housed children from all over the North, children whose parents were dead or, for a number of reasons, were unable to care for them.

And now they were going to try and send her there. And it was all her fault. She was the one who had told the women everything. But she had thought they might help her to go home to *Kōhkom*. They had tricked her. So kind and caring, and look what they'd done to her. The tension in the other room seeped through the wall and settled around Melanie so tightly she couldn't breathe. She pressed closer to catch her mother's low terse reply. "I can take care of her," Frances said.

Melanie hung onto the doorknob, every nerve, every muscle taut. Doris' words seared into her brain, until she was ready to scream at her to shut up.

"I know you're doing the best you can," Doris

said. "But right now you're not in a situation to give her the care she needs. At the residence she'll be well fed, her health will be taken care of, and warm clothes will be provided. Then, when you have some furniture and money, you can come and get her." She paused. "In the meantime, you'll be able to visit her and take her out as often as you like. It'll only be for a short while – say two or three weeks."

There was quiet. Melanie waited. Desperate to know what was happening she opened the door a crack. She heard Doris say, "Will you at least think about it? I'll leave my number with you."

Her mom didn't answer. Melanie bit the fist she held to her mouth. Then, like a spring wound too tight, she leaned against the door frame and sobbed into an old blanket. Now she was sure she would be taken away.

Finally she heard her mother speak. "I'll think about it … I'll let you know."

Melanie made no effort to wipe her face. She watched Doris write down her number and give it to Frances. Doris hesitated as she walked to the door. "Frances," she said, "I'm not trying to scare you, but if Melanie continues to go to school hungry and without warm clothes, Social

Services may step in. Then she'll have to go to a foster home, and it will be a lot harder to get her back."

Melanie saw her mom close the door and lean against it. She knew from the heaving shoulders that her mother was crying. She sidled into the room and leaned against the wall, clutching the blanket around her and glaring at her mother as she moved heavily away from the door.

Frances held out her arms to comfort Melanie but Melanie slapped and kicked at her. "Don't touch me," she bawled, "I heard what you said."

But kicks and slaps weren't about to drive Frances away. Melanie fought her mother's arms, and with each surge of strength she vowed, "I'll run away. I'm not going there."

Over and over Frances crooned, "Nobody's going to take you away …" until at last, soothed by the hypnotic sound of her mother's voice, Melanie began to believe the words. The two clung together and cried till there were no tears left.

Later, as Melanie lay on the quilts in the crook of her mother's arm, she confessed. She had no choice; she was sick about what she'd done. "It's all my fault," she said, starting to cry again.

"Hush, my girl, of course it's not your fault." Her mom, trying to console her, hugged her close.

"Yes, it is." Melanie kicked viciously at the blankets. She sat up and looked at her mother, tears streaming down her face. "I told the ladies everything. I made it seem worse and I told them we didn't have any furniture or anything."

She waited for her mom to yell at her, but there was only a long silence. "I'm sorry," she finally whimpered when her mother didn't speak. "I didn't mean to … I didn't know…."

Melanie heard her mother sigh. Then she felt her mom's fingers wind through hers, and her mother's free hand stroked her hot forehead. "I didn't realize how much you missed home, my girl. I thought you were just being stubborn. I guess I learned something here too. I just can't take you away from *Kōhkom* after all these years and expect you to think of me as your mother just like that. It'll take time." She sighed again.

"But you are my mother," Melanie replied in a tiny voice.

"Yes, but *Kōhkom*'s been more of a real mother to you than I have." She laid her chin on Melanie's black hair. "Maybe I was wrong to take you away from home."

Melanie sniffled. "Can I go back to *Kōhkom* for a little while, so they won't take me away? I promise I'll come back whenever you want me too." She held her breath waiting for her mom to answer. A hiccup escaped.

"Yes, I think that might be best."

Melanie drew her legs up to her chest and twisted her body so that she could see her mother. "Can't you come home too?"

Frances stirred. "I wish I could, my girl. But I started this and I have to finish it." She laid a kiss on Melanie's forehead.

It was a long time before they settled down to sleep.

Melanie went back to school in the morning. Rachel looked at her, long and hard. "What's wrong?" she asked, linking her arm through Melanie's.

"I might be going back home," Melanie said, her voice shaking.

Rachel's face darkened. She stopped walking. "What happened?"

Melanie tried to stall her. "I'll tell you after school."

"No, tell me now." She pulled on Melanie's

arm and steered her away from the bridge.

Melanie told her how the women from the school came to Lorraine's house and about Doris' visit. "And it's all my fault," she confided to Rachel, eyes brimming all over again at the horror of what she'd done. "Now they blame my mom for everything and want to send me to the residence or a foster home."

Rachel hugged her. "You didn't know, Melanie."

Melanie wiped her eyes. She drew a shaky breath. "So my mom said I could go back home with *Kōhkom*."

"But I'll miss you!" Rachel wailed.

"I'll miss you too," Melanie replied. "You know when I blew out the candles on my birthday cake? Well, I wished I could see *Kōhkom* and Keena. But I never thought it would be like this."

The two girls walked toward the school, arms entwined. Just before the entrance door Melanie's face brightened. "Guess what?" she said, and continued before Rachel could say a word. "You can have the bottle back, and you can send me a message in the spring."

Rachel managed a wan smile. "Spring is months and months away. You'll forget all about me by then."

Melanie stood still. "Pinkie promise," she said, holding up her little finger. "We'll write each other every week."

Rachel curled her little finger around Melanie's. "Pinkie promise."

"Anyway," Melanie added, "I mightn't be going right away."

When she entered the classroom Miss Ryan smiled and welcomed her back. Melanie felt the teacher's eyes linger on her. All day she tried to think of how to tell the teacher she was leaving.

Finally, after school, as Miss Ryan gave the girls some scraps of coloured paper to take home, Melanie mustered her nerve. "Teacher, I might be leaving," she said, as fast as if it were all one word. She held her breath, waiting for the questions she knew the teacher would ask.

Miss Ryan's concerned eyes searched her face. "Leaving?" she echoed, holding the paper in front of her. "How come?"

Melanie couldn't meet her teacher's eyes. "The school is making too much trouble," she mumbled, looking away.

"Oh, Melanie," was all Miss Ryan said. She reached out a hand towards Melanie, then withdrew it and ran it through her short hair. Her cheeks reddened as if they'd just been slapped.

She opened her mouth to speak then closed it again, searching for words. Finally, she said in a faltering voice. "What did we do?"

Melanie's reply was no more than a whisper. "You said that my mom wasn't taking care of me, that I was hungry," she said, her eyes on the bag she held open for the paper.

The teacher laid a gentle hand on Melanie's shoulder. "Oh, Melanie, I'm so sorry. I didn't mean to make trouble. I was trying to help."

Melanie looked into Miss Ryan's eyes. "I know, teacher," she said. If the teacher had tried to touch her or hug her, she knew she wouldn't have pulled away like she had on her first day of school here.

Miss Ryan's voice matched her sad face. "If you go, when will you leave?"

Melanie found that for a second or two she couldn't trust herself to speak. She was having strange feelings, like she almost didn't want to go any more. She shrugged. "Maybe in a few days."

Miss Ryan was persistent. "Where will you go?"

"Back to Elk Crossing, to live with my *Kōhkom*."

Miss Ryan looked like she had when she'd read the class the sad part in the book about the boy who lived with his grampa and the grampa had a stroke.

Melanie looked directly into her teacher's blue eyes, as blue as the river back home. The teacher didn't need to feel sorry for her. Melanie knew she belonged in Elk Crossing with *Kōhkom*, more than she would ever belong here in the city. "It's okay, teacher," she said, "I like living with my *Kōhkom*."

Leaving

*M*elanie went to school the next day and the next, which was Halloween. She didn't figure there was any way she'd be able to dress up this year. There certainly weren't any old clothes lying around the house, other than what they wore every day. And money was scarcer than blueberries in January. It didn't matter; Halloween costumes were for little kids.

But Rachel didn't agree. "You're coming home with me at lunchtime to get ready," she said. "Even my mother goes to the costume party at her school."

So that's what they did.

But Melanie didn't have to depend on Rachel after all to rustle up a costume for her. The evening before Halloween her mother dragged her over to Victoria's apartment, where Victoria dug out an assortment of potential put-togethers and accessories, and threw them all across her bed for Melanie to decide which she wanted.

"It was just like shopping at a store, except everything was free," Melanie told Rachel, as she lugged the green garbage bag holding her stuff down the steps to Rachel's place.

She dumped her bag onto her friend's bed, next to Rachel's witch costume. She picked up the scraggly black wig and tried it on. She and Rachel giggled. "I have to take good care of it," Rachel said. "When we come back from trick-or-treating my mom is wearing it to her party."

The girls headed to the bathroom where Rachel teased Melanie's hair so that it stuck out all around her head. Rachel shook a can of blue spray. "I used this last year," she said. "Close your eyes." Melanie's hair stiffened as fast as wet clothes hanging outdoors in winter. Next, Rachel dipped into the make-up Victoria had given Melanie and put a moon-wash blue shadow around Melanie's eyes and a peach blush on her cheeks. Melanie giggled and completed the effort by smearing her lips with a plum shade, while Rachel did her own face.

Then she pulled on a faded blue denim

miniskirt, which she belted snug about her waist, and a pair of black heeled boots also belonging to Victoria. With several strings of beads of varying shades and lengths her outfit was complete. Preening in the bathroom mirror, she flashed a smug grin. She looked as good as any rock star in the school was likely to look today.

She wheeled around from the mirror when she saw Rachel, in full costume, behind her. "Are you ever witchy!" Melanie squealed. She ducked around her friend and ran from the bathroom screaming as Rachel advanced on her, brandishing long, claw-like fingernails.

Rachel called after her, through fits of laughter. "We'd better hurry, or we'll be late."

They helped each other shrug on their coats, carefully so as not to disturb their costumes. There was no time to eat. Anyway, lunch was the last thing on their minds as they hurried back to school, eager to inspect everyone else's costumes.

Melanie and Rachel joined the bunch of kids hanging around the front entrance, impatient for the afternoon to begin. Their noisy chatter about the parade that would take place in the gym, and the classroom party after, was more like a shouting match than anything else. No one noticed the car at the edge of the playground, just a few metres away. But when the blaring horn drowned out their loud voices, everyone turned and saw Tanya look back at the car.

Tanya's mother, her sandy-coloured hair frizzed just like Tanya's, hung her daughter's jacket out the window and yelled, "Tanya, you get over here and get this coat!"

Tanya continued to walk away from the car, her chin stuck out like a rock ledge. Defiant and daring, she looked back over her shoulder at her mother.

The voice from the car rose to a scream, while the coat dangled from the window. "If you don't come here and get this jacket, there'll be no Halloweening for you this evening, young lady."

Tanya's step faltered. She turned around, her green eyes spitting defiance, and dragged her feet back to the car.

The girls gawked, all eyes glued to Tanya and her mother.

Tanya grabbed her jacket, sputtered words they could only guess at, and stomped toward the front door of the school.

Melanie stared too. But it wasn't because of Tanya's fight with her mom. Melanie hardly noticed that. Her horrified eyes raked over

Tanya, taking in every detail of the girl's costume. Tanya's outfit was an exact copy of Melanie's, from the stiff blue hair right down to the black boots. Desperate to escape, Melanie darted futile looks toward the school door, but it was still locked. And her other clothes were at Rachel's apartment. She edged back behind her friend and hunched down, praying that no one else would notice.

Tanya did, however. She pushed past them, but stopped on spotting Melanie, glaring at her out of glassy, green mascaraed eyes, like those of a store mannequin. For once, she had nothing to say.

Melanie met her look. She thought she saw a twitch in that rigid face and the eyes looked a little too shiny. It was as if a layer of protective nastiness was crumbling, exposing Tanya's bitter disappointment. Melanie saw in the eyes she faced more than a little of herself.

She hesitated, breathing in jagged, uneven breaths. Then, "Hey," she said, putting her hand up to her mouth like a microphone, "we can be a band." She screwed her face into a smile and danced over to Tanya, as if they'd been best friends forever.

Melanie was keenly aware that everyone was watching … and waiting.

For a long minute Tanya didn't move or speak. Her suspicious eyes darted from face to face and finally settled on Melanie. She blushed under her makeup, and with a shrug of her shoulders she dropped her coat and met Melanie halfway. The two admired each other's hair and clothes. "We even have the same beads, almost," Tanya said, swinging hers around in her hand.

Later, on their way home from school, Rachel said, "I can't believe how nice she was. It must be a Halloween spell." She tittered at the idea.

Melanie said, "She asked if I wanted to go trick-or-treating with her."

"Did she?"

"But I told her that we were taking your little brothers around the neighbourhood."

Rachel's mother pulled into her stall as the girls crossed the parking lot. "She came home early this evening so we could take the boys out before it gets dark," Rachel said.

Later, after trips to the bathroom and drinks, the girls trotted down the street each with a twin in tow. The boys wanted to eat each treat right away and couldn't understand that they had to wait for their mom to check their bags first. Having tramped two blocks they'd had enough and were loudly demanding to get at their bags. Rachel and Melanie decided they had had enough too and marched the boys home.

Then they set off on their own. Two hours later, cold as corpses, teeth chattering, they shuffled homeward. They thawed out over bowls of scalding noodle soup until finally their fingers were nimble enough to pick through the piles of treats they dumped on opposite ends of the kitchen table.

Melanie waited at Rachel's place until Mrs. Settee dropped her off on the way to her own Halloween party.

"That's enough candy to treat a whole village," her mother said when Melanie walked in the door. Her mom always said Halloween was better than Christmas for some kids; each had as much junk as the other.

Melanie guzzled two glasses of water; the sunflower seeds were really salty. Her mother shook the treats out of her bag onto the counter, a handful at a time. She sifted through, picking out a caramel for herself.

"Did anybody come to our door?" Melanie asked, wiping her mouth with the back of her hand and reaching for a stick of licorice.

Frances peeled off the thin plastic wrapper

and popped the caramel into her mouth. "Not since I got back."

"Where were you?"

"Doris stopped by and we went for coffee."

Melanie froze. "What did she want?" She didn't like this Doris any more. It was sneaky of her to come around when she knew Melanie wouldn't be home.

"She wanted to know what we decided…."

"What did you tell her?" Melanie locked fearful eyes on her mother.

Frances cupped Melanie's pinched face in her warm hands and brought it close to hers. She rubbed Melanie's nose with her own, saying, "I told her I'm sending you home to your *Kōhkom*."

Struggling to free herself so she could question her mother more, Melanie planted her hands on her mom's shoulders and pushed her away. "What did she say then?"

Frances' hands dropped to her sides and she pulled her sweatshirt down over her hips. She leaned against the counter and brushed Melanie's tangled hair back off her face. "She said there's a residence van leaving in the morning to pick up two kids at Birch Point, and you can catch a ride."

"In the morning?" Melanie echoed. "When we wake up?" She frowned at her mom. "That's not enough time for anything."

Frances crossed her arms, her eyes intent on Melanie. "It's up to you," she said. "If you don't want to go tomorrow, I'll go phone Doris and tell her."

"Phone her tonight? From where?"

"The corner store. It's open until eleven."

Melanie's eyes pleaded with her mother. "What do you think I should do? Do you think I should go?"

"I can't decide that for you, my girl. You have to make up your own mind."

"If I don't go tomorrow, when will I go?"

"I don't know. Doris didn't know of any other trips in the next while. I suppose I could send you by bus...."

"Is the van ride free?"

Her mother nodded.

Melanie made up her mind. She didn't want her mom having to find money for a bus ticket. "I'll go," she said, looking at the candy on the counter without much appetite any more. Pushing the treats into a pile she asked her mom, "Can you do a favour for me?"

Without waiting for a reply she left the

kitchen, returning immediately with the bottle Rachel had given her. "Can you give this back to Rachel? She knows all about it."

Frances chuckled. "Why do you want to give her a bottle?"

"In the spring she's going to send me a note in it."

Frances raised her eyebrows. "Oh?"

"Yeah, she'll drop it in the river and I'll get it in Elk Crossing. The river goes right to Elk Crossing, you know."

"Hmm, I see."

"You have to promise."

"I promise," Frances said, wrapping her arms around Melanie. "I'm sure going to miss you, my girl."

"Me too," Melanie said. And she meant it.

"You go have a bath while I pack your clothes. I don't want you going home to *Kōhkom* like that. She'll ask you if that's the way girls in the city wear their hair."

Melanie giggled and laid the bottle on their box table so her mother would be sure to see it.

Later, bathed and packed, she cuddled close in her mother's arms on the quilts. "*Kōhkom* doesn't even know I'm coming."

"Yes, she does. I phoned her tonight and told

her you'd be going either tomorrow or sometime soon."

"What did she say?"

"She said now she would be able to sleep well again."

"She really wants me?"

"You know she does – you're her sleeping partner," her mother teased.

Melanie smiled in the dark, fleetingly. Neither of them spoke for a few minutes.

Then Frances said, "I can't believe you're really going. Are you happy?"

"Not as much as I thought I would be."

"What do you mean?"

"Well, I'm glad I'm going to see *Kōhkom*. But I don't want to leave you – and Rachel." Melanie snuggled her chin on her mom's soft upper arm.

"Yeah." Her mom sighed. "Nothing ever works out the way you expect."

Melanie wished she could say goodbye to Rachel. In her mind she carried on an imaginary conversation – what she would say and what Rachel would say. Maybe she'd be able to run over to Rachel's real quick in the morning before the van came. She'd get up as soon as her mom called her.

But Melanie woke long before her mother's call – from a dream about Rachel and the bottle. Rachel was about to throw the bottle into the river when she slipped. The bottle rolled out of her hand and down the bank till it disappeared. The dream was so real Melanie scrambled off the quilts and into the living room to see if the bottle was still on the box. It was. She brought it to bed with her but couldn't sleep, even though she forced her eyes to stay shut.

She heard the train cars clank and bang as they changed tracks, right in her back yard it seemed, and when the guy next door pulled out of his driveway she shook her mother's arm. Frances sat up with a start and squinted at the clock radio Victoria had lent them. The ghostly green hands pointed to six twenty-two. She yawned and stretched. "We'd better get up. The van's coming at seven."

"I guess there's no time to say goodbye to Rachel?" Melanie asked, without much hope of being allowed to.

Frances shook her head. "It's too dark. Besides, the van'll be here before long."

Melanie washed and dressed, surprised at the twinges of excitement that stirred in her chest. In spite of her mom's lonely face and despite having to leave Rachel without saying goodbye, Melanie couldn't help looking forward to seeing *Kōhkom*. And pictures of the river and her rock flitting across her mind made her feel even guiltier.

She let her mom take as long as she liked braiding her hair.

Melanie stood in front of the window and watched for the van while Frances brushed and braided, making each stroke of the brush a caress and cradling each handful of hair like a keepsake.

"When will you give the bottle to Rachel?" she asked.

Frances took Melanie's hair elastic out of her mouth and passed it to Melanie to hold. "I'll bring it to Victoria's with me this evening, and phone Rachel to come pick it up."

Melanie felt satisfied.

Promptly at seven the yellow van braked in front of their house and a short, robust man tapped on the door. "I'm Willy," he told her mom, grinning widely. His brown face crinkled as he joked, "Is there a package here for me?"

He tossed her bag into the van and pretended he was going to toss her in too.

Melanie giggled.

But her mother's laugh was a broken one. She kissed Melanie again and again. "Be a good girl.

Help *Kōhkom* as much as you can."

Melanie nodded.

Another kiss. "Don't make her worry about you."

Melanie blushed, remembering how she'd made her mother worry. She squeezed her mom's neck. "I'll be good, I promise. You ask *Kōhkom* when you talk to her." She was crying when she climbed into the van.

Willy shook Frances' hand. "Don't worry, Missus, I'll take good care of her," he said, and tweaked Melanie's braid.

Melanie clutched her bag of Halloween treats. She had taken out all the caramels, her mother's favourites, and left them on the counter. She waved as the van pulled away from the curb.

Looking back, Melanie saw Frances follow them into the street, her outstretched arm still reaching out as they turned the corner and drove out of sight.

Home

The van rolled onto Diefenbaker Bridge. City-bound traffic crawled through the early morning dark. Its sleepy speed made Melanie think the drivers wished they were lucky enough to be going the other way.

Willy sailed by them, in a northbound lane that was as empty as a snowmobile trail in spring. Melanie glanced out the side window, then cupped her hands around her eyes and leaned against the cold glass for a better look. "There's the river," she said, feeling her heart beat a little faster.

"Yep," Willy said. "Pretty well frozen up now, most places I'd say." He drove off the bridge, following the straight stretch of highway east along the river bank.

Melanie knelt on the seat and fixed her eyes on the ribbon of ice, white except for occasional dark splashes that meant open water. The bottle should float along here without snagging on anything, she thought. "Are we going to follow it all the way to Elk Crossing?" she asked Willy.

"Huh? You mean the river? Not all the way. We'll meet up with it every now and then."

"Do you have a map?"

"Sure do." Willy opened the glove compartment. Melanie lurched forward and managed to grab a pair of sunglasses, a wrench, and an unwashed plastic coffee mug before they clattered to the floor. Willy pulled some things out and shoved others aside until finally he produced a tattered and coffee-stained highway map of Saskatchewan. He passed it back to Melanie. "Is this what you're looking for?"

"That's it," Melanie said. Except for the mess it was in, the map was just like the one Miss Ryan had lent her. She spread it across her lap and smoothed out the wrinkled paper as much as she could. Then she folded it so that only the route from Prince Albert to Elk Crossing showed. As the river curved away from them she said to Willy. "We'll meet up with it again at Nipawin, right?"

Willy pulled out to pass a pulp truck. "How come you're so interested in the river?" he asked, without taking his eyes off the highway.

"It goes by our house in Elk Crossing. The same river. In the summertime there's even a pipe that brings water from there right into *Kōhkom*'s kitchen." Melanie pored over the map again, noting that Nipawin and Dumont Dam were the two places where the river met the highway.

Later that morning as they crossed the long green bridge a few kilometres outside the town of Nipawin, Melanie smiled with satisfaction. The river was even wider here than in Prince Albert. Their bottle would do just fine. And when Willy cruised by Dumont Dam she glimpsed the same wide white streak.

Melanie settled back in her seat, barely noticing the bumpy northern dirt road. She didn't mind the seven-hour drive at all. She jumped out to stretch her legs when Willy stopped at a gas station and sipped on the Pepsi Willy bought her while she daydreamed about wading into the river to reclaim her bottle.

Shortly after two o'clock Melanie leaned forward in her seat to read the green provincial highway sign up ahead on the right. "Elk Crossing," she said, in the loud voice of a television

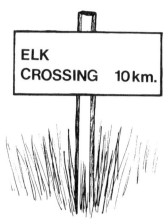

announcer. She giggled when Willy tooted the horn several times, as if there were a wedding or something.

Willy steered far to the right to negotiate a turn. "Elk Crossing is just around this bend and up the road a bit," Melanie said. Unable to sit still any more, she tugged at the seatbelt strap to loosen it and then wiggled forward until she sat at the very edge of her seat.

"Are you sure?" Willy asked, straight-faced. He chewed lazily on the toothpick between his teeth. "I thought we still had at least twenty kilometres to go."

Melanie ignored his teasing. "No, it's right up ahead." She jabbed her finger at the wind-shield. "See that sign? Jimmy Skye painted it."

Melanie remembered when Jimmy finished it two springs ago. Her class had even walked here one afternoon to see it. She looked at the proud elk with its huge antlers spreading across the backgound of wide blue river flanked by leafy green trees and read the hand-painted lettering. *Wāwāskesiw Āsoganihk.* "That's the Cree name," she said, feeling as proud as the elk in Jimmy's sign looked. "Now we're on the reserve," she announced, "and there's where Jimmy lives, the first house."

Willy slowed the van and looked out his window. He whistled an old country tune Melanie recognized. She noticed his mouth was tucked into an easy smile. He drove down the straight stretch of reserve road as unhurried as a midsummer tourist.

Between the road and the river lay wooden bungalows, too small for the large families they held even before they were built. They were strewn haphazardly along the way like a child's building blocks dropped and forgotten, their once bright colours weathered and drab. Strings of clotheslines decorated the yards like old Christmas streamers, as full and sagging as the homes behind them.

While she still sat on the edge of her seat, Melanie was no longer in any hurry. She knew the road, with its dips and potholes, like a trapper knows every twist and turn of his trapline. And she knew every house. Driving past them was like turning the familiar pages of a family photo album and knowing each friendly face within.

"Old Uncle Joe … he's ninety-six … lives in that blue house all by himself. He still cuts his own firewood," she told Willy.

Willy nodded, still whistling.

"And there's Musher Sol's house. He wins races all over the North. He's got lots of trophies all over his house."

She pointed out the store, the church, the nursing station, the school, and Auntie Elsie's place. Then, her seatbelt snapped back and she gripped the door handle, impatient to show Willy where *Kōhkom* lived. When Willy looked for a good place to pull off the road she stood up as if she'd jump out while the van was still moving. Willy quickly came to a stop.

He had barely stepped on the brake when the door of a small, yellow bungalow with an un-painted porch swung open and *Kōhkom* hobbled down the worn, wooden steps, her moccasins scuffing the hard, black earth under her thick brown-stockinged ankles. Melanie leaped from the van, leaving the door swinging wide, and ran up the path.

Kōhkom wore the red print cotton housedress Melanie and Frances had given her at Christmas last year, and over it a navy blue sweater that had seen better days. Like most of the elderly women on the reserve, her hair – still black – was done up in two braids which fell down the front of her sweater. Her round face wrinkled into a smile that made Willy smile too.

Kōhkom gathered Melanie to her, engulfing her in the smell of smoked fish, simmering berries, the wood stove, and a hundred other aromas that Melanie hadn't even known she'd missed.

Melanie hugged back, snuggling into *Kōhkom's*

arms as if nestling her head against a soft cosy pillow. Her arms tightened around her grand-mother's wide waist; even a crowbar couldn't have pried her loose.

Willy had collected her jacket and bag from the van and laid them on the step. Melanie, one arm still around her grandmother, shook the hand he held out first to her and then to *Kōhkom*.

Kōhkom said, "Melanie, *iskwēsis, nāta wîsakî mina.*" Her grandmother spoke perfect Cree, better than Willy, who threw in English words here and there.

Melanie ran inside and returned with a jar of cranberries, which *Kōhkom* pressed into Willy's hand before he left.

When she'd gone to get the berries Melanie noticed some strange clothes hanging in the porch, kids' clothes. Once Willy left she lost no time asking *Kōhkom* whose they were.

Kōhkom put another stick of wood in the stove. "Florence and the children are living here," she explained.

Melanie was not pleased. "How come?" she asked.

"Pierre and Elsie thought I should have someone here. They think I'm too old to live by myself." She set the cover back in place. "They just moved in a little while ago."

"How come you didn't tell Mom on the phone?"

Kōhkom made no reply and the set of her wrinkled face told Melanie she wasn't about to. Melanie figured she knew though. *Kōhkom* didn't say much of anything over the phone. And she probably thought Frances would worry that something was wrong with her.

"Where's everybody now then?"

"The children are in school and your auntie works at the store."

Melanie had to bite her tongue. Her aunt had not only taken her mom's place in *Kōhkom*'s house but she had taken her mom's job as well.

She prowled about the kitchen, out of sorts. She touched everything, to make sure nothing had changed. She even ran her hand over the woodbox in the corner and had to pull out a sliver of wood that stuck in her skin.

Kōhkom coaxed her to have some lunch.

"I'm not hungry, *Kōhkom*," she insisted. "I ate lots on the way here."

Finally *Kōhkom* threw up her hands and said, "*Ē hē, ki pāwanān!*" Then she poured hot water on the used teabag in her mug and straightened the cushion on her hard-backed chair before settling herself close to the stove.

She set her mug down on the open oven door and asked Melanie to bring her beading basket. *Kōhkom* rummaged around and pulled out a small brown paper bag, which she held out to Melanie. "For your birthday," she said. She took Melanie's outstretched hand in hers and pressed the open palm to her mouth before laying the bag in it.

Suddenly Melanie was ashamed of her feelings. No matter who moved in, she would always matter to *Kōhkom*. Melanie felt *Kōhkom*'s kiss spread all through her. But it was the look in *Kōhkom*'s eyes that made tears in her own, not the mad kind she had cried when she had gotten angry at her mom in the city, but soft, sweet ones. Still she didn't want her grandmother to see her. *Kōhkom* might think the tears were because her life had been so bad in the city, or because she didn't want her cousins living there. She bent over *Kōhkom* and gave her a fierce hug, like she never wanted to let go, ever.

Kōhkom rubbed Melanie's back, as she'd always done when Melanie needed her to. Melanie closed her eyes, knowing for sure she was home. Finally, the teary spell passed and she stood up.

She opened the bag and took out a beautiful, beaded barrette. Her heart skipped a beat. The dream. This was the barrette, the one she hadn't been able to see in her dream. Raising her eyes to her grandmother's face she said, "*Kōhkom*, I had a dream about this barrette, but I couldn't see it."

Kōhkom smiled wisely, "Now you can, *no sisim*"

Melanie's eyes lingered over each detail. The barrette was about as big as *Kōhkom*'s coin purse, with blue beads on the outside, then white, and in the middle tiny beaded flowers of the palest pink. "Oh, *Kōhkom*, thank you," she breathed, "it's so beautiful."

Kōhkom nodded, smiling with pleasure. "Turn around," she said, "I'll put it in your hair."

Melanie knelt on the floor while her grandmother pinned her braid. She closed her eyes, and felt as good as she had in the dream. She hugged *Kōhkom* again before running to the tiny, white-framed mirror on the wall by the table, where she knelt on a chair and twisted back and forth to see the back of her head.

"I wish I could show Rachel," she said, still looking into the mirror.

"Who's Rachel?" *Kōhkom* asked.

So Melanie sat on the end of the table, feeling her barrette every so often, and told *Kōhkom* all about Rachel and Victoria, but not about Doris or Tanya. Now and then she felt the smooth beads and stood up to tilt her head every which way in the mirror. In between she told *Kōhkom* about the river, but not about the goose or getting wet. *Kōhkom* would be mad.

When she finished telling *Kōhkom* everything she could think of, she said, "I'm going down to the river before Jenny and Danielle get home, okay?"

Kōhkom nodded and shuffled to her feet to lay another stick of wood in the stove.

With her jacket wide open, Melanie raced down the narrow trail. She stared upstream toward Prince Albert as far as she could and studied the river's path until she was forced to shield her squinting eyes from the glint of sun on new ice. She turned toward the rock and blinked. But it didn't help. As watery-eyed as if she'd been swimming all afternoon, she climbed her rock.

She could have found those toeholds with her eyes closed, but she took her time. She stretched her arms wide and held on tight, hugging the rock as she hoisted herself up, and laying her face against it, just as she had lain on her grandmother's bosom a short while ago. She gazed up the river for a long time straining to see as far as she could, as if she could see the whole length of it.

Return

She had been sitting on her rock looking at the river for a while before she heard her cousins, Jenny and Danielle, tearing down the path. Not wanting them here right now she jumped off and ran to meet them.

First they visited Keena, who hugged Melanie so hard her neck was sore after. With Keena along they visited the neighbours on either side, and then on their way to see Uncle's new snowmobile, they stopped in to see Auntie Elsie. Melanie was wrapped in Auntie's strong arms and felt like she was home all over again. Auntie Elsie gave them bannock, hot from the oven. Melanie ate it, remembering the first evening at Victoria's apartment. The thought crossed her mind that when she was in the city she kept remembering the way it was here and now that she was here she was remembering things in the city.

By dark they had made the rounds of the tiny community. Jenny and Danielle, hungry and cold, ran ahead of them towards home. Melanie and Keena strolled along as though out for a walk on a summer's day, instead of the dark frosty evening it was. Melanie's eyes lingered on the tall spruce making a black line along the road on either side. "In the city I couldn't stay out at night like this," she told Keena.

Keena looked at her. "How come?"

"Too dangerous." Melanie sniffed the air and looked up, searching the sky for a spiral of smoke. She wondered who was smoking meat. She loved the smell.

"You mean somebody could grab you, like this?" Keena said, clutching her suddenly around the shoulders.

Melanie, head still in the air, jumped and they both laughed.

"Was it awful having to live there?" Keena asked, linking her arm through Melanie's.

Melanie drew in her breath. "At first it was," she said. "But it wasn't so bad after a while." She kicked a rock out of her path.

"Then how come you came home?"

"Well, my mom thought it would be better until she gets some furniture and stuff for our house."

Keena stopped dead and pulled Melanie to a halt with her. "You mean you'll have to go back?"

"If my mom wants me to. It's lonely there for her all by herself. But if I do go back it'll only be until Mom finishes school. Then we'll both come back here." This time she tucked her arm in Keena's. "Now come on – I'm freezing."

Lying in *Kōhkom*'s bed that night, waiting for her grandmother to finish her cup of tea, Melanie thought about her conversation with Keena. Without thinking about it much at all she had told Keena that she would return to the city if her mom wanted. Had she meant it? Thinking about her mother all alone tonight in the empty house, she realized she did.

Finally, *Kōhkom* settled next to her. "Did you like the city?" she asked.

Melanie didn't answer right away. As last she said, "Not really. I might have liked it better if everybody was there with me."

Kōhkom chuckled. Melanie felt her grandmother's comforting arm drawing her close. She curled up into a ball, feeling as safe as a kitten in

Kōhkom's strong protective arms. But as her eye-lids drooped and her body relaxed, she thought of her mom, all alone, and even *Kōhkom* couldn't protect her from the ache that gnawed at her insides.

When she woke in the morning *Kōhkom* had already heated water on the stove for Melanie and her cousins to wash before school. After a breakfast of tea, bannock, and jam she tramped along the river road to school with Jenny and Danielle. *Kōhkom* had found a warm jacket for her to wear. Melanie didn't know where it had come from. It didn't matter.

Walking into the old clapboard building where she'd spent all her school days, except for the past few weeks, wasn't at all like the first day of school at McKenzie Community School. Friends crowded around her, curious to know what it was like to go to school in the city. Melanie shrugged. "It was okay," she said, "but I'd rather be here." She even got her old desk back and sat down rubbing her hand across it, just as she had touched everything in *Kōhkom*'s kitchen.

She slipped easily back into Cree and the freedom of life in the tiny community. Her days were full of school, fun with her cousins, and evenings with *Kōhkom*. And whenever she could, she sat alone on her rock by the river thinking about her mom, and Rachel, and Victoria.

Kōhkom was teaching the girls beading and they practiced in the evenings on scraps of moosehide. Melanie hoped to be able to bead a pair of moccasins that *Kōhkom* was sewing her mom for Christmas.

She hadn't realized how much she would miss her mom and checked for a letter on Monday, the first mail day since she'd come home. There was nothing. And on Thursday the only mail was *The Northern Telegraph*. But the following Thursday there was a brown package addressed to Melanie Bluelake. It wasn't in her mother's handwriting, though.

Right in the store where they got their mail Melanie tore open the box. It held all her supplies, even her pencil crayons. She pulled out a large sheet of paper which had been folded over and over again. She opened it, and there was the biggest letter she had ever seen. Her classmates had written on chart paper, the kind they always used to write stories together in school. She hurried home and spread it out on the table to read.

McKenzie Community School

November 12

Dear Melanie,

Rachel said your mom told her you went home to Elk Crossing. We're sorry we didn't get to say goodbye to you and we want you to have your supplies.

We miss you. We made cards for you. Maybe some day you can come back to our school.

> *Yours truly,*
> *Miss Ryan's Class*

Melanie removed her stuff from the box and found the cards underneath. Most of the boys had drawn pictures of cars and spaceships on their cards. Rachel drew a picture of the river, with a goose taking off from the water. On its body Rachel had printed *Canada*. Melanie laughed. There was a bottle in the river too, with the words *message inside* printed on it.

There was a card from Tanya too. She had drawn a picture of Melanie and her in their rock star costumes. Melanie laughed when she looked at it. She had also stuck a sticker at the bottom where she'd signed her name. It was a shiny one of the sun peeking out from behind a silver cloud.

The next day in school Melanie wrote a letter back.

A week later a letter did arrive from her mom. She wrote that she missed Melanie and that she was smart in school, just like Melanie was. She said that Doris told her she'd heard that there was a nine-month computer training program starting in Island Rapids the following September. She was going to work hard to finish her grade twelve so she could apply.

Auntie Florence had read the letter aloud. Melanie took it from her and danced around the kitchen kissing it. "Island Rapids!" she shouted. "That's hardly any distance at all from here." They all laughed at her.

In the letter her mom also asked Auntie Florence to put her name on the waiting list at the band office for a house of their own. She said she would be home for Christmas December 20.

Melanie pulled a chair over to the wall and stood on it to count off the days to Christmas on the calendar. Only twenty-nine days to go! She'd better get started on those moccasins. And maybe she'd ask *Kōhkom* to bead a pair of earrings for her mom to take back to Rachel.

After supper she planned to sneak away to her rock. She had lots to think about, and she could think better there than anywhere else in the world.

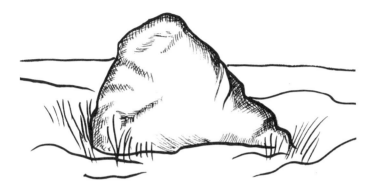

Glossary of Cree Words and Expressions

ēhē	yes
ēyako-ōma	this one
iskwēsis, nāta wīsakīmina	go get the cranberries, girl
kinanāskomitin	thank you
ki-nēhinawāncī	do you speak Cree?
kinipa	hurry
ki pāwanan	you're skinny
kōhkom	grandmother
mōnīyās	white man
mosōm	grandfather
Melanie awa	this is Melanie
nēwo	four
niso	two
nisto	three
nitānis	my girl
niyānan	five
no sisim	little one
pēyak	one
tānisi	hello
tē pakōhp	seven
waniska	wake up
Wāwāskesiw Āsoganihk	Elk Crossing

Glossary Note:

For matters of consistency, the publisher has used the Saskatchewan Indian Cultural College's Cree translations. In this instance they have used the N–Dialect, recognizing that there are also Y– and TH–Dialects and that translations are dependant on the individual Cree communities.

About the Author

Betty Fitzpatrick Dorion was born in New-foundland in 1952, and finished her B.A. and B.Ed. there at Memorial University. She then spent time on two reserves in Saskatchewan, and since 1979 has been a teacher in Prince Albert, where many of her students are of Indian and Metis background. She is the mother of two teenagers. *Melanie Bluelake's Dream* is her first book.

About the Illustrator

Sherry Farrell Racette is an artist and educator. She has been painting, drawing and making things since she was little. Sherry received a Bachelor of Fine Arts and a Certificate in Secondary Education from the University of Maitoba and later, a Masters in Education from the University of Regina.

A member of the Timiskaming Band of Algonquins in Quebec, Sherry was born in Manitoba and has been involved in Indian and Metis education for many years. She is currently an assistant professor with the Faculty of Education, University of Regina.

Sherry wrote and illustrated *The Flower Beadwork People* for the Gabriel Dumont Institute and recently illustrated Maria Campbell's *Stories of the Road Allowance People* (Theytus Press).

More stories for young readers from Coteau Books

The
by N

Wh᠎   ʏear-
old   ling?
Poll   ᠎ the
mys᠎   inter
Isab   n to
poin᠎   new
resp   h at-
tent᠎   ᠎r.
ISB᠎

Pell᠎
by ᠎

San᠎   ty, is
forc᠎   ᠎ve to
the ᠎   ᠎ndra
goes   ᠎ican.
Wh᠎   ᠎uth,
San᠎   ᠎ the
long prairie winter.
ISBN 1-55050-049-X   \$4.95 trade pb   112 pages